grk
DOWN UNDER

Other books by Josh Lacey

grk
DOWN UNDER

Josh Lacey

Andersen Press · London

First published in 2010 by
ANDERSEN PRESS LIMITED
20 Vauxhall Bridge Road
London SW1V 2SA
www.andersenpress.co.uk

This edition published in 2013

British Library Cataloguing in Publication Data available.

ISBN 978 1 84939 739 1

Typeset by FiSH Books, Enfield, Middx.
Printed and bound in Great Britain by
CPI Group (UK) Ltd, Croydon, CR0 4YY

Chapter 1

He was trapped.

He couldn't escape.

They had slammed the door and turned the key in the lock, abandoning him here in this small, cold, dark cell.

He didn't know why.

He was being punished. He knew that much. But he didn't have a clue what he had done wrong.

It wasn't important. Only one thing mattered now. Escaping. He had to get out. He had to get home. And he had to do it as fast as possible. He didn't want to spend another wasted minute inside these drab, dismal walls.

He paced around the cell, inspecting his surroundings, searching for a way to escape. He tapped the cold concrete floor, then scraped the walls, hoping to find a crack or an opening, but the bricks felt solid and immovable. The ceiling was too high for him to reach. He rested his shoulder against the door and pushed with all his strength, but the lock didn't budge.

He noticed that the hinges were covered in scratches. The floor and the walls too. Bite marks lined the bars of the cell.

Others must have been here before him. They too had tried to escape: scratching and biting and digging, exhausting themselves with the effort. But they had failed.

He suddenly understood that he would fail too.

He was fit and muscular, but he couldn't dig through a concrete floor or reach a ceiling that was many times his own height.

His teeth were strong, but they would be shattered by those thick steel bars.

He would be stuck here for ever. He knew that now. He would have to spend the rest of his life in this small, dark, miserable cell.

Despair overwhelmed him. He threw back his head and howled – a long, agonising howl, expressing all his sadness and pain and desperation.

To his surprise, his cry was answered immediately. All around him, yelps and shouts came back, expressing desperation and pain and sadness just like his.

He wasn't alone.

The cells were packed with prisoners.

Their stories were identical to his. Male and female, young and old, they had been abandoned here.

He listened intently to their barks and shrieks, hoping to gain some new information, but they told him nothing that he didn't already know.

Grk lay down on the floor, put his head on his paws and stared at the bars of his cell, wondering what to do.

He had to escape from here and find his way back home.

But how?

Chapter 2

It was a sunny morning in the mountains and hundreds of hikers were setting out for hearty walks through the Alps, clasping sticks and carrying knapsacks packed with provisions. Snow covered the mountaintops, but the lower valleys were lush, green and speckled with flowers.

Thirty thousand feet above them, an Alitalia flight cruised through the air. One or two passengers looked out of the windows at the mountains below them, staring at the sculpted peaks and crevices. The others were too busy sleeping, working, talking, playing games, watching movies or reading books. All of them had their own lives, their own worries, their own fears, their own reasons for travelling from London to Rome on a Friday afternoon. But we're not interested in any of them. We're just interested in a man, a woman and a boy sitting near the back of the plane.

The man was reading the *Daily Telegraph*. The woman was flicking through the pages of *Vogue*. And the boy was arguing with her.

He had been arguing with her all morning. He started arguing when she woke him up. He continued arguing while they had breakfast and finished packing their bags. He even argued with her in the car on the way to the airport.

In fact, the same argument had been continuing for more than three weeks now.

'It's so unfair,' said Tim for the thousandth time. 'You can't put Grk in prison.'

'He's not in prison,' replied Mrs Malt. 'He's just staying in a kennels for a couple of nights.'

'A kennels is a prison for dogs,' said Tim.

'Don't be ridiculous,' said Mrs Malt. 'Cuddles Kennels has been recommended in all the best guides. Grk will have much more fun than he does at home. He'll be surrounded by lots of other lovely dogs. Anyway, he's only going to be there for a couple of nights and then he'll be back with us.'

Tim could hardly believe what he was hearing. 'Would you want to spend two nights in prison? Of course you wouldn't! No one would! It's so unfair. Why can't he come to Italy?'

'Because he can't,' said Mrs Malt. 'You saw the invitation. Children are welcome, but pets aren't allowed.'

'If Grk can't come, then I don't want to go either.'

'You don't want to stay in a lovely hotel? And eat lots of yummy spaghetti?'

'Not without Grk,' said Tim. 'I'd rather turn round and go home.'

'Well, you can't.'

'Why not?'

'Because we're already halfway there. And even if we weren't, you couldn't stay in the house on your own.'

'Why not?'

4

'Because you're not old enough to look after yourself.'

'Why not?'

Mrs Malt sighed. 'We've talked about this for days and I don't want to talk about it any more.'

'Why not?'

'Because ... Because ... Because ...' Mrs Malt glanced at her husband, hoping for some support, but he was reading the business pages of the *Daily Telegraph* and hadn't heard a word of their conversation. Mrs Malt turned back to her son. 'We're not going to talk about this any more,' she said in a firm voice. 'I want you to keep quiet and read your book till we get there.'

'But—'

'No buts! I don't want to hear another word out of you, Tim. Will you please just sit quietly and read your book.' Mrs Malt opened her magazine and, pretending that she was entirely alone on the plane, studied a photograph of a skinny woman in a flowery dress.

Tim sighed.

It was so unfair.

Why wasn't he allowed to stay at home? Why did he have to spend the weekend with his mum and dad? When would he be old enough to look after himself?

He knew there was no point asking any of these questions. His mother had made up her mind and she wasn't going to change it.

Anyway, she was right.

They were already halfway to Italy and the pilot wasn't going to turn the plane around just to rescue a lonely little dog.

They would be landing in Rome soon. They would take a taxi to the centre of the city, where they would stay the night in a hotel. Tomorrow, they were going to a wedding. One of Mr Malt's oldest friends was marrying an Italian woman. It was guaranteed to be really boring. Tim had been to three weddings and they were always really boring.

When the wedding was over, they would have to stay one more night in the hotel. And then, finally, they would be allowed to catch another plane back home and rescue Grk from Cuddles Kennels.

Tim sighed again.

Poor Grk!

Right now, he would be lying in his cage, wondering why he had been abandoned so cruelly.

He wouldn't understand what had happened. He'd think that they had gone away for ever.

I'm sorry, Tim said silently to himself. He knew Grk couldn't hear him, but he wanted to say it anyway. *I'm very, very sorry. We've locked you in a prison and you must be miserable.*

But just wait. Be patient. We're only staying in Italy for the weekend. As soon as this boring wedding has finished, we'll be flying back again. And then, finally, you can come home.

Chapter 3

At seven o'clock on Friday evening, the door of Cage 73 swung open and a red-faced man staggered into the cell, carrying a heavy bucket in each hand. He was wearing big black boots, dirty jeans, an old blue shirt and thick rubber gloves. His name was Trevor Cuddle and he was the owner of Cuddles Kennels.

Trevor Cuddle started the kennels with his father, Arthur, and his wife, Marjorie, and they'd been running it for almost fifteen years. In that time, they hadn't just looked after thousands of dogs. They had also taken care of cats, rats, newts, salamanders, anacondas, ferrets, guinea pigs, gerbils and just about every other pet that you can imagine – feeding and exercising them while their owners went on holiday.

Trevor Cuddle closed the door behind him and stared at the small white dog curled miserably on the cold concrete floor. Then he unfolded his print-out of every animal currently resident at Cuddles Kennels. He ran his finger down the list of numbers until he reached 73.

CAGE: 73
NAME: Grk
SEX: Male
BREED: Unknown
OWNER: Malt

'Grk,' said Trevor Cuddle. 'Never come across that one before. Foreign, is it?' He glanced at the dog as if he was expecting an answer. 'How are you meant to say it, then? Gruk? Grook? Grrrrrok? Come on, then. Give us a clue. How do you like your name to be said?'

Some dogs might have barked. Others would have wagged their tails. Grk simply stayed on the floor and stared at Trevor Cuddle with a stern expression.

'Not very chatty,' said Trevor Cuddle, 'are you?'

This time, he didn't bother waiting for a response. From one of his buckets, he filled Grk's bowl with fresh water. From the other, he tipped out a few tough, brown biscuits.

'There's your dinner,' he said. 'Hope you enjoy it.'

Most dogs couldn't wait for their food. They jumped up and started scoffing as soon as the biscuits landed in their bowl.

Grk didn't move a muscle. Food had lost all meaning for him. He just lay on the floor, his head on his paws, hardly even twitching his nostrils to sniff the biscuits.

'Let me give you some advice,' said Trevor Cuddle. 'You won't get fed again till tomorrow morning. If I was you, I'd eat the lot.'

His words had no effect. The little dog stayed on the floor, his ears flat against his skull, a picture of misery.

'Oh, dear,' said Trevor Cuddle. 'You're not sick, are you?'

He hoped not.

Sick dogs made trouble for him. He'd have to phone

the vet or, even worse, interrupt the owners on their holiday. He might have to waste his whole morning on a single animal. And he didn't have a minute to spare; the kennels was packed with animals.

A second glance reassured him. He could see that the little dog didn't actually look ill. No, there was a much simpler explanation for its sad eyes, tired legs and limp tail.

Over the years, Trevor Cuddle had learned a lot about dogs. He could recognise happy dogs, sad dogs, angry dogs, aggressive dogs, difficult dogs and dangerous dogs. Looking at Grk, he knew immediately that this was a dog suffering from depression. The poor little pooch missed his owners.

'Don't worry,' said Trevor Cuddle in a kind voice. 'You're only going to be here for a couple of nights. It'll pass in a flash. Come Sunday, you'll be heading home. Now, eat some biscuits and drink some water and you'll soon feel better.'

Trevor Cuddle stepped out of the cage, locked the door and walked down the corridor to the next dog. If he hadn't been so busy, he'd have chatted to the depressed dog for a few minutes, or even taken him for an extra walk around the yard, but he didn't have time for lengthy conversations with other people's pets. This weekend, his cages held eighty-three dogs, eleven cats, two hamsters, a family of cockatoos and a rather scary snake named Graham. Before Trevor Cuddle could go back to his house and have his own supper, he had to give food and drink to every single one of them.

When the man in the big black boots had locked the cell and retreated down the corridor, Grk took a couple of sips of water and nibbled at the biscuits, but didn't finish them.

He couldn't eat.

He was feeling too gloomy.

He hated this cell.

He loathed being locked up.

He wanted his freedom.

He wanted to smell fresh air and walk on the pavement and roll on the wet grass and choose which tree to pee against.

More than anything, he wanted to be back home.

Grk was a small dog with beady black eyes. He had white fur with black patches and a perky little tail. When he was happy, his tail wagged quickly back and forth. But when he was miserable, as he was right now, his tail drooped sadly between his back legs and trailed along the floor.

His small brain was working hard, trying to work out how to escape, but he couldn't come up with any good ideas.

He lay for a long time, frowning and thinking and listening to the squeals and barks of the other dogs around him, wondering when he would be rescued. What had happened to Natascha? Where was Tim? Why had they left him here? Didn't they care about him?

Every few minutes, he pulled himself to his feet and wandered around the boundary of his cell, sniffing the walls and scratching the floor, but nothing had changed.

No secret doorways had opened. No cracks had appeared. There was no way out.

He lay down on the floor again and wondered if he was going to be here for the rest of his life.

Grk was used to spending his nights in a small, cosy basket, lined with thick cushions. If he woke up with a dry throat, he could pad into the kitchen and take a few sips of cool, clean water. If he heard any strange noises, he would go and investigate, but his nights were usually quiet and peaceful. From dusk till dawn, he stretched out on his comfy cushions and slept.

A night in the kennels was very different.

Grk's bed was a concrete floor. He had a bowl to drink from, but the water was warm and brown. The night was punctuated by strange noises echoing all around him.

He could hear other dogs in the other cages. Some yelped, others howled and a few whimpered. One barked desperately for hours. Another whined softly and miserably, calling for her owners, asking where they had gone and why they had abandoned her here.

Every few minutes, an aeroplane roared overhead, taking off or landing at the airport. The whole building shook with the noise. Glass trembled in the windows and the walls wobbled.

That night, Grk didn't get much sleep.

Chapter 4

Tim was right. The wedding was boring. In fact, that Saturday afternoon was one of the most boring afternoons of his entire life.

The ceremony went on for hours. The dinner lasted even longer. Tim had to sit at a long table with the other children. Most of them were Italian, so he couldn't understand what they were saying. Some spoke English, but they didn't bother saying much more than 'Hello!' or 'Good morning!' or 'My name is Fabio!' He wished he'd been allowed to bring a book. Or, even better, stay at home with Grk.

Max and Natascha were lucky to miss it.

As you probably know, Tim lived in London with Max and Natascha Raffifi. They were Grk's original owners and their parents were dead. If you want to find out how they all came to be living together, you should read *A Dog Called Grk*.

Anyway, Max and Natascha had been invited to the wedding in Italy too, but they couldn't come. They had a good excuse: they were in Stanislavia, a small country in Eastern Europe, not far from Russia. They were staying with their cousins, who lived in the country's capital, Vilnetto.

Stanislavia had changed. Colonel Zinfandel, a cruel dictator, was dead and the country had been freed from his rule. (If you want to discover exactly how he died, you should read *Grk Takes Revenge*.) Now Max and Natascha had gone back there for a quiet holiday, enjoying some good Stanislavian weather and some ordinary Stanislavian food and some pleasant Stanislavian conversation.

They would have taken Grk too, but one of their cousins was violently allergic to dogs. Put her in the same room as a dog and her skin immediately erupted in a bright-purple rash. If she had to spend a night in a house with a dog – even a dog as small and polite as Grk – she'd almost certainly end up in hospital, breathing oxygen through a tube. So Max and Natascha left Grk in London with Tim and the Malts.

Natascha didn't like the thought of Grk spending even a single night in a kennel, but Max told her that he'd be fine.

'Grk can look after himself,' said Max. 'He won't let the other dogs bully him. You know what he's like. He'll just have a nice quiet weekend on his own, eating lots of biscuits and dreaming about rabbits.'

'I hope you're right,' said Natascha.

'Of course I'm right,' said Max. 'I'm always right.'

But this time, he wasn't.

Chapter 5

Grk was ready.

It was breakfast time. He could hear footsteps.

Grk lay down on the floor and placed his head on his paws.

Twice a day, Trevor Cuddle came down the corridor with a pair of buckets. He stopped at every cell, delivering food and water to the dogs. Once a day, Marjorie Cuddle, Trevor's wife, or their daughter, Jean, took the dogs for a walk.

Grk could hear shrieks and howls of anticipation. Up and down the corridor, other dogs were scratching the bars of their cages, wild with excitement, desperate to get their teeth clamped around some biscuits.

He listened to the footsteps and the yowls and the barking and the jangling keys and the rattling biscuits. These sounds were repeated again and again. Then he saw Trevor Cuddle stopping outside his cell.

As always, Trevor was wearing big black boots, dirty jeans, an old blue shirt and thick rubber gloves. He was carrying a bucket of water in his left hand and a bucket of dog biscuits in his right hand.

'Morning, Groooook,' said Trevor. 'How are you today?'

Without waiting for an answer, Trevor put the buckets on the floor, reached down to his leather belt and unclipped a large ring of keys, one for each cage in the kennels. He sorted through the ring, searching for Number 73.

Trevor turned the key in the lock, clipped the ring back on his belt, picked up his buckets and stepped into the cage.

'Breakfast time,' he said. 'I hope you're hun—'

A white flash sped between his big black boots.

'Wha—?' cried Trevor Cuddle.

He was talking to himself. Grk was already sprinting down the corridor, past barred doors and locked cages, ignoring the shouts and barks and squeals that pursued him.

Trevor shouted at the top of his voice: 'Hey! Grroook! Come back here, right now, this minute!'

Grk took no notice. He turned the corner and disappeared from sight.

Trevor Cuddle reached down to his belt and grabbed his walkie-talkie. He switched it on and brought it to his mouth.

'Escape in progress!' he yelled. 'Culprit is proceeding along Corridor 3 and heading for the North Door. Escape! Escape! I repeat: we have an escape!'

Grk sped down the corridor.

On either side of him, dogs darted forwards, hurling themselves at the bars of their cages. Bloodhounds, beagles, borzois, schnauzers, spaniels, salukis, collies, corgis and chihuahuas – they all wanted to join him. Their yelps and cries urged him onwards, willing him to outwit the Cuddles.

Grk would have liked to stop and say hello to every dog he passed. But there wasn't time for chitchat. He just had to run.

He didn't know where to go, of course.

Nor did he know what he would do when he got there.

He didn't have a car. He couldn't catch a bus or a train. Maps meant nothing to him. The route from Cuddles Kennels to his own comfy basket was long and complicated. Even if he managed to get out of the kennels, there was very little chance that he would ever be able to find his way back home.

Grk didn't worry about any of that.

He just ran.

Five people worked at Cuddles Kennels: Trevor Cuddle; his wife, Marjorie; his father, Arthur; his daughter, Jean and Jean's boyfriend, Ibrahim.

On an ordinary Sunday morning, the five of them would work for a few hours, sweeping cages, filling bowls with biscuits and walking dogs around the yard, then have a big lunch together.

But there was nothing ordinary about this particular Sunday morning. A message came through the walkie-talkie saying, 'Escape! Escape! I repeat: we have an escape!'

Marjorie was peeling potatoes in the kitchen. She threw down her peeler, dropped a potato in the sink and ran into the yard, leaving the half-prepared lunch on the kitchen table. It would have to wait till she came back again. An escaped dog was much more important than their stomachs.

Ibrahim was sweeping the basement storeroom. Dropping his broom, he grabbed a couple of leather leashes and a muzzle from their hooks by the door, then sprinted up the stairs.

Jean was crouching in a cage, tickling the ears of a melancholy spaniel named Percy. Hearing the message on her walkie-talkie, she whispered, 'Don't worry, Percy. I'll be back in a flash.' Then she stood up, let herself out of the cage, locked the door and hurried into the yard.

Percy pressed his nose mournfully against the bars of his cage, wondering when he might get his ears tickled again.

Arthur was enjoying a quiet doze on the sofa. He sat up with a jolt and stared at the walkie-talkie on the floor, wondering if he'd been dreaming. Or was he going mad? Was that walkie-talkie really talking to him? Then he recognised the voice coming from the speaker. He rubbed his eyes, rolled off the sofa and went to see what all the fuss was about.

Trevor was waiting for them in the yard.

'I've lost him,' he cried. 'I've lost that darn dog!'

'Which dog?' asked Marjorie.

'Grook. Or Gruk. You know who I mean. The one with the silly name.'

'Half of them have silly names,' said Arthur. 'I don't know why people can't just call their dogs Rover or Blackie, like they did in the old days. I remember when—'

'Not now, Dad,' said Trevor. 'We've got to move fast. In the history of Cuddles Kennels, we have never lost a single dog. I want to keep that one hundred per cent record one hundred per cent intact. Let's split up. We'll search the whole place. Marjorie, you take the North Corridor. The South Corridor is yours, Ibrahim. I'll take the East Corridor and Jean can do the West. Dad, secure the house and check the storeroom. You never know where this mutt might be hiding. If you see him, report your location immediately on the walkie-talkie. If not, we'll meet back here in fifteen minutes. Any questions?'

There were none. They hurried in different directions.

The yard was empty. The kennels were quiet. Nothing moved.

Nothing, that is, except a single sparrow fluttering through the air and darting across the gravel, searching for crumbs.

And the nostrils of a dog.

The nostrils belonged to Grk. He was hiding in the shadows. He had been lurking there, watching Trevor, Marjorie, Jean, Ibrahim and Arthur. Now they had gone, he was wondering how to get out.

Cuddles Kennels was surrounded by a high brick wall. The only exit was a tall steel gate and it was shut.

Grk was trapped.

He might have escaped from his cage, but how was he ever going to get out of the kennels?

Then his nostrils twitched.

And twitched again.

18

He could smell something that interested him. He wasn't quite sure what it might be, but he was absolutely convinced that he wanted to find out. Keeping himself hidden in the deepest, darkest shadows, Grk went to investigate.

Chapter 6

Tim sighed.

He was ready to leave. He had been ready for a long time. Early this morning, he sprang out of bed, got dressed and packed his suitcase.

Then he waited for his parents.

And waited some more.

They slept for two hours longer than him.

When they finally emerged from their room, they spent ages eating breakfast.

Mr and Mrs Malt sat on the terrace, savouring their cappuccinos and their croissants and their glasses of freshly-squeezed orange juice, leaning back in their chairs and enjoying the sunshine.

Tim sat with them, but he didn't enjoy the sunshine. Or the croissants. Or the orange juice. Or anything else. He just wanted to grab his bags and get out of there.

'We could go to the airport early,' he suggested. 'They might be able to put us on a different flight.'

Mrs Malt said, 'Would you like another croissant?'

'No,' said Tim. 'I'd like to go home.'

Mrs Malt turned to her husband. 'How about you, Terence? Another croissant?'

'Why not?' said Mr Malt. 'When in Rome...'

Mrs Malt laughed.

Mr Malt chuckled too and gestured for the waiter.

Tim couldn't see what was so funny. Didn't they know that a dog was in prison? Didn't they understand that every minute wasted here was another minute of agony for Grk?

He tapped his feet impatiently on the paving stones, wishing they would hurry up, and wondered what Grk was doing right now.

Eating? Sleeping? Or whimpering softly to himself and wondering why he had been abandoned?

Tim reached into his pocket and pulled out a brochure. It was a promotional leaflet advertising the benefits of leaving your pet at Cuddles Kennels. On the front of the brochure, big yellow letters said:

WELCOME TO CUDDLES KENNELS

There was a photograph of a dachshund, a labrador and a beagle trotting cheerfully across a patch of sunlit grass. Tim must have read the brochure a hundred times, but he read it again anyway.

CUDDLES KENNELS –
a happy hotel for your pet!

While you're lying on a beach or eating a romantic dinner in a delicious foreign restaurant, your dog or cat will be having a holiday of his own!

For the past fifteen years, Trevor Cuddle and his
family have been caring for animals, providing pets
with a home from home. We guarantee their happiness!

Clean cages! Good food! Long walks! Reasonable rates!

That's why pets love Cuddles!

On the back of the brochure there was a small map
showing that Cuddles Kennels was located just outside
the boundary of the airport. If you were catching a
plane, you could drop your dog at the kennels and drive
to the airport's entrance in a couple of minutes.

The Malts had left Grk at the kennels on Friday
afternoon. They would be back from Rome on Sunday
afternoon. Grk would have to stay in the kennels for
only two nights and less than three days.

Tim folded up the brochure, tucked it in his pocket
and told himself to stop worrying.

His parents were right.

Grk would be fine.

What could go wrong in two nights and three days?

Chapter 7

The Cuddles combed the kennels for clues.

Trevor, Marjorie, Ibrahim and Jean hurried along the North, South, East and West corridors, inspecting every cage.

Meanwhile, Arthur Cuddle hauled his weary old bones down the stairs and into the storeroom in the basement. Huffing and puffing, he pulled aside the tins of dog food and peered behind the sacks of dog biscuits. Finding nothing unexpected, he locked the storeroom, climbed the stairs and searched the house.

The bedrooms were empty. The bathrooms too. So was the sitting room. If the dog had been here, he'd gone by now.

Arthur stood in the hallway, wondering what to do next. He could go and join the others, of course. He could help them in their search. Or he could sneak into the sitting room, lie down on the sofa and have a quick nap.

Hmm, that was a tempting thought. It had been a busy morning. He could use a little rest before lunchtime.

Arthur tiptoed into the sitting room, hoping his son wouldn't catch him, and lay down on the sofa. He was just pulling a blanket over his legs and arranging the cushions when he heard a peculiar noise.

What was that? And where was it coming from?

He could hear snuffling and growling and scraping and ripping.

As if a pair of dogs were fighting. And one of them was tearing the other apart.

It seemed to be coming from the kitchen.

Arthur threw the blanket aside, jumped up from the sofa, hurried down the corridor and charged into the small, cosy kitchen. And then he stopped, his eyes blinking in astonishment, scarcely able to believe what they were seeing.

A small white dog was squatting in the middle of the kitchen table. His front paws rested on a leg of lamb, his teeth had just torn out a tasty chunk.

'That's our lunch!' cried Arthur.

All week he'd been looking forward to his Sunday lunch. It was his favourite meal. No contest. Succulent roast lamb with crunchy roast potatoes, a handful of boiled carrots and some tasty redcurrant jelly. What could be nicer than that?

Now it had been torn to pieces!

And swallowed into the belly of a small dog with a stupid name!

Without pausing to think, Arthur reached for the nearest implement. His fingers clasped around the handle of a potato peeler. 'Come here, you little mutt!' He raised the peeler into the air and rushed forwards.

Grk whirled round.

Arthur lunged.

PRAAAANNG!!!!!

The potato peeler plunged into the tabletop. If Grk hadn't jumped out of the way, he would have been skewered.

Arthur grabbed the peeler with both hands, pulled it out of the tabletop and hurled himself after the little dog.

Grk was already rushing out of the door. He found himself in the hallway. To his left, he saw the front door. It was closed. Some dogs can open doors, turning the handles with their paws, but Grk wasn't one of them. To his right, he saw two more closed doors and a flight of stairs. Behind him, he heard heavy footsteps and a roar of rage. Grk galloped up the staircase to the first floor.

'Come back here, you miserable mongrel!' yelled Arthur, pounding up the stairs in pursuit. 'I'll show you what happens to dogs who steal other people's lunches!'

At the top of the stairs, Grk didn't even hesitate. He just raced into the nearest bedroom. And realised, immediately, that he had made a terrible mistake. There was no way out.

And now Arthur Cuddle was standing in the doorway, blocking the only exit. Grk was trapped.

With an evil grin on his face, Arthur took two steps forward and made a mad swing with the potato peeler.

Grk dodged out of the way.

Arthur swung again.

This time, the peeler missed Grk by a millimetre. Any closer and he'd have lost an ear.

Arthur swung once more.

Grk could see that there was only one option open

to him. It was dangerous. It might even be deadly. But he had no choice. If he was going to survive, he had to do it. He sprang into the middle of the bed, bounced on the mattress and launched himself out of the open window.

His paws scrabbled in the empty air, searching for something to hold. His head turned desperately from side to side. His ears flapped. His tail waggled. And he landed with a loud THUMP on the grass. He rolled over, picked himself up and started running.

Back in the house, Arthur Cuddle leaned out of the window, shaking his fist and yelling at the top of his voice. Grk couldn't hear what he was saying and he didn't care either. He just wanted to get away from Cuddles Kennels. Without knowing where he was going, let alone what he might do when he got there, he ran across the grass.

He dodged round trees and scrambled through bushes and darted across a main road. Cars hooted and a motorbike swerved desperately to avoid him, but Grk took no notice. He just kept running.

For a minute or two, he ran along the side of a tall fence, and then he arrived at a hole, which must have been made by a fox or a rabbit. Grk wriggled through this bunny-sized gap, emerged on the other side of the fence and carried on running.

The grass beneath his feet turned to tarmac. He passed long hangars and parked trucks and several enormous aircraft. And then he stopped.

What was that smell?

Sniff, sniff, sniff.

Mmmmmmmmmm.

Sausages!

Grk was a sensible dog. He didn't want to be guillotined by a potato peeler. Nor did he wish to spend the rest of his days locked inside a small, dark cell. He knew he had to run and run and run and run and run and run and keep running till there was no chance that the Cuddles could catch him.

But he did love sausages. Lamb or pork, beef or chicken, plain or spicy, he didn't mind. He loved them all. And, right now, he could smell the most deliciously sausagey scent that had ever wafted past his nostrils.

All thought of the Cuddles vanished from his mind. In fact, his head was empty of anything except sausages. For the past couple of days he had been too depressed to eat. He had hardly even touched the hard biscuits that passed for food in the kennels. But he was feeling much more cheerful now – and much hungrier too.

He lifted his nose into the air. His little black nostrils quivered.

There! That was them! The sausages were buried in that pile of suitcases.

Grk didn't pause to wonder who owned the suitcases or why they were stacked on the back of a truck. He just trotted across the tarmac, sprang aboard the truck and delved into the suitcases, searching for the one that contained those majestic sausages. The scent grew stronger. He was getting closer. He urged himself onwards.

27

When the truck suddenly shuddered forwards and drove across the tarmac, Grk didn't even notice. Nor did he care when the truck stopped and two men in luminous jackets started loading the cases into the bowels of an aircraft. Grk simply followed the source of the smell, leaping out of the truck and into the luggage compartment of a Boeing 747. He was followed by a barrage of suitcases, building a wall behind him. When every piece of baggage had been loaded aboard, the door closed with a loud clunk.

Grk raised his head and looked around.

He couldn't see anything. His whole world had been plunged into darkness.

Oh, well. He didn't need his eyes. His nose would do. Guided by the unmistakeable scent of those sausages, he continued his search.

Grk burrowed into the suitcases until he found the one he wanted. It was a large blue bag secured with a silver zip.

Suddenly the whole world roared and shook.

Grk took no notice. The rest of the world could look after itself. He just wanted to get his jaws around those sausages. Gripping the suitcase with his front paws, he gnawed at the zip.

The engines roared again.

The plane shuddered slowly forwards.

The zip unzipped with a satisfying rip and Grk thrust his head into the suitcase.

Socks rolled one way. Shirts flopped another. Books fell out and flapped open. Grk dug through T-shirts, tights, skirts and blouses till he found a bulky bag at the bottom of the suitcase. He punctured the plastic with his sharp little teeth.

As the plane eased into the air, Grk chomped happily through half a kilo of best British sausages.

Chapter 8

The flight from Rome was delayed for an hour and fifteen minutes. When they finally landed, the Malts had to wait forty minutes for their luggage. Collecting the car took another half hour. By the time they were finally driving out of the airport and heading for Cuddles Kennels, Tim was horrified to realise that they were almost two hours late. He said, 'Can't you drive any faster?'

'I'm afraid not,' said Mr Malt. 'Unless you want me to crash.'

'I don't mind.'

'If we crashed, we'd have to wait for the police. And probably the ambulance too. Then we wouldn't get to see Grk for hours.'

'Fine,' said Tim. 'Don't crash. But can you just get there as fast as possible?'

'Of course I can,' said Mr Malt. He signalled left, turned off the main road and drove down a narrow lane shaded by tall trees. A large wooden sign said WELCOME TO CUDDLES KENNELS. Mr Malt pressed the bell and announced his name. When the tall steel gates opened, he drove into the yard and parked the car.

Trevor Cuddle was waiting for them. 'Good afternoon,' he said. 'How was your flight?'

Mr Malt smiled. 'Very nice, thank you.'

'Did you have a good holiday?'

'It was lovely,' said Mrs Malt. 'Thank you.'

Tim said, 'Where's Grk?'

'Ah-hah,' said Trevor Cuddle. 'That's how you pronounce his name. I had wondered.'

'Where is he?' asked Tim.

'Where is who?' said Trevor Cuddle.

'Grk,' said Tim.

'Oh, yes,' said Trevor Cuddle. 'Grk. Your dog. You probably want to see him, don't you? Well, the thing is . . . ' And then he paused.

'Yes?' said Tim. 'What's the thing?'

'The thing is . . . ' Trevor Cuddle rubbed his hands together and searched for the right words to say. 'Now, please don't take this the wrong way, but I have to inform you that there has been an incident.'

'An incident?' said Tim. 'What sort of incident?'

'This would be much easier if we all kept calm,' said Trevor Cuddle. 'There's no need to overreact. We're all friends here. Why don't you come inside and have a nice cup of tea?'

Tim wasn't interested in tea. 'What's happened? Is Grk safe? What have you done to him?'

'How about a biscuit?' said Trevor Cuddle. 'Or some toast with jam? You must be starving after your flight. We've got some lovely biscuits. Come inside and have a nice cuppa.'

'I don't want tea,' insisted Tim. 'I don't want toast or biscuits either. I just want to know what's happened to Grk. What have you done to him?'

31

'I haven't done anything,' said Trevor Cuddle. 'He did it himself.'

'Did what himself?'

'I've been running these kennels for fifteen years and we've never lost a single animal. But your dog... Your Grk... He's the first.'

'You've lost him?'

'Oh, no. We haven't lost him. You can't pin the blame on us, my young friend. As I just said, your dog did it to himself.'

'Are you saying he escaped?'

'He did indeed.'

'But how?'

'He broke out of his cage. Then he jumped out of a window. And we haven't seen him since.'

'Haven't you been looking for him?'

'Of course we have. Non-stop. Myself and my family have searched the entire vicinity. We've alerted the police, the neighbours and every relevant organisation for miles around. You don't have to worry, my young friend. We'll find him. As you must be aware, Grk is not a large dog. And he has very short legs. He can't have got far.'

Chapter 9

Thirty thousand feet above the ocean, the Boeing 747 cruised through the air, carrying four hundred and sixteen passengers halfway around the world. They left London at ten o'clock in the morning. Twenty-one hours later, they would finally touch down in their destination. During that time, four hundred and sixteen passengers ate and slept, watched movies and read books. Four hundred and sixteen passengers peered out of the window, watching the clouds and the sky. Four hundred and sixteen passengers wriggled in their seats, trying to get comfortable, or roamed along the aisles, exercising their weary muscles. Four hundred and sixteen passengers signalled to the stewards, asking for another blanket or a glass of orange juice. Four hundred and sixteen passengers pressed the buttons on their seats, adjusting the lights or the heating, or tipping their chair backwards, making themselves more comfortable.

The four hundred and seventeenth passenger didn't have lights or heating, books or movies, food or drink. He felt even more cramped and restless than any of the four hundred and sixteen people in the cabin above him, but he couldn't lean backwards or adjust his chair to make himself more comfortable. In fact, he didn't even have a chair. He was squatting in darkness in the luggage compartment, wondering when someone would come and rescue him.

Grk was cold, hungry and thirsty.

He had finished the sausages long ago and now his stomach was beginning to wonder when the next meal would arrive. He was desperate for a drink, but he couldn't find any water. And, worst of all, he was cold.

Very cold.

Colder than he had ever been in his entire life.

When the plane climbed above the clouds, the temperature dropped. At first, Grk had hardly noticed. All his attention was focused on the sausages. He chomped them and chewed them and gulped them down, never pausing to wonder if he should keep some for later.

When he finished them, he sat back and licked his lips.

That was when he noticed the temperature.

Thirty thousand feet above the Earth, the air is extremely chilly.

Grk snuggled into the depths of the suitcase, burying himself among someone's clothes, wrapping his body in a pile of T-shirts, but he still couldn't get warm. After a few minutes, he started shivering. He whined and moaned, but no one came to help him. So he threw back his head and howled at the top of his voice, hoping he would be heard by Tim or Natascha or Max or someone, anyone, who would come and rescue him.

WHHHOOOOOAAAAHHH!

His howls echoed through the darkness.

WHHHOOOOOOOOOOOOOOOOAAAAAAAAAAHHH!

Four hundred and sixteen passengers were sitting just above Grk, separated from him by a ceiling and a floor and a few metal struts. All four hundred and sixteen of them were enjoying hot food and cool drinks and the latest movies. Not one of them heard the mournful cries of a desperate little dog, down in the luggage compartment, begging for help.

Minute by minute, Grk's cries grew fainter, but he refused to give up.

He was sure someone would help him. They always did.

Right now, Tim would be hunting for him. Natascha would be knocking on doors, asking if anyone had seen a runaway dog. Max would be running through the streets and calling his name.

Inspired by the thought of his owners, Grk opened his mouth and tried to bark for help, but he was so chilly and exhausted that he could only manage a pathetic little yelp.

Whooah!

When they reached Singapore, Grk was lying at the bottom of the suitcase, silent and scared and very, very cold. Some time later, the whole world rumbled and lurched again. Grk sunk further into the pile of clothes and shivered.

Chapter 10

They searched until nightfall. Arthur Cuddle led the Malts to the patch of grass where Grk had landed when he jumped out of the window. There, they split up and went in different directions.

Tim and Mrs Malt checked the edge of the field and walked through the trees, calling Grk's name, listening for an answering bark.

Meanwhile, Mr Malt walked along the road, checking the verges, searching for any evidence of an accident and hoping he wouldn't find it.

On the other side of the road, Mr Malt could see the tall fence that marked the boundary of the airport, but he didn't bother searching there. Grk might be mischievous and energetic, but he wasn't a superdog. He couldn't possibly climb over such a tall fence.

It was possible, however, that Grk had turned round and sneaked back into the kennels, so the Cuddles checked the entire premises once again, turfing animals out of cages, peering under beds, peeling back carpets, hunting through cupboards, opening fridges, emptying bins and looking anywhere that could possibly conceal a small dog.

By dusk, no one had located any trace of Grk. He seemed to have completely disappeared. Tim wanted to stay the night in Cuddles Kennels, so he could start searching again at dawn, but Mr and Mrs Malt insisted on taking him home.

'We've been travelling all day,' said Mr Malt. 'I'm shattered. I'm sure you must be too.'

'I feel fine,' said Tim.

'I've got a good idea,' said Mrs Malt. 'When we get home, we could have a takeaway for supper. That would be a nice treat, wouldn't it? What would you like? Pizza, Chinese or Indian?'

Tim shrugged. 'I don't care.'

'How about a nice chicken korma from the Taj Mahal?'

'Fine,' said Tim. 'Whatever.'

They drove home.

When they got back to the house, Mr Malt carried their suitcases upstairs. Mrs Malt rang the Taj Mahal and ordered a delivery. Tim waited till she'd finished, then called Max and Natascha.

Had he ever made a more difficult phone call?

If he had, he couldn't remember it.

He dialled the number of their cousins in Vilnetto. A voice answered in a language that he couldn't understand.

'Hello,' said Tim. 'Do you speak English?'

'Only when I have to.'

Tim laughed. 'Hi, Max. How are you?'

'Not too bad. We're just having supper. You should be here, Tim. You could try some good Stanislavian cooking. None of that tasteless British rubbish.'

'I like British food,' said Tim.

'That's because your tastebuds have been ruined by years of eating it. Hey, let's talk about something else. I don't want to make you feel bad about your national cuisine. How's life? How's Grk?'

Tim paused for a moment, searching for the right words. 'That's what I wanted to talk to you about. Something's happened.'

'What do you mean? Something serious? Is he OK?'

'I hope so,' said Tim. He described how Grk had escaped from Cuddles Kennels and explained the efforts that he, his parents and the Cuddles had been making to find him. 'Will you tell Natascha?'

'Of course I will,' said Max. 'But I'm sure she'll want to talk to you herself. Can you wait a second? She's in the next room. I'll go and get her.'

Tim waited for a minute or two. Down the phone line, he could hear the distant sound of two people talking in Stanislavian. He recognised their voices: Max was speaking slowly and calmly, relaying the news about Grk, and Natascha was interrupting him with lots of questions, her voice high-pitched and anxious. The voices stopped. Tim heard footsteps and then Natascha picked up the phone.

'Is it true?' she said. 'Has he really disappeared?'

'I'm afraid he has,' said Tim. For the second time, he explained exactly what had happened. To his surprise, Natascha didn't interrupt him once, but simply listened in silence, absorbing every scrap of information about her beloved dog.

Chapter 11

'G'day and welcome to Australia! As you can probably see through the windows, the sun is shining and it's a beautiful afternoon here in Sydney. The temperature outside is a very pleasant 28 degrees Celsius. That's 82 degrees Fahrenheit. If you want to adjust your watches, it's currently 17.10 here in Sydney. For those of you who prefer old-fashioned ways of telling the time, it's ten-past five in the afternoon. You can switch on your phones, but please don't call your friends and family back in London. Back there, it's very early in the morning and they'll probably be fast asleep. We will be disembarking very soon, but the captain has requested that you remain in your seats until the seatbelt signs are switched off. We'd like to remind you that smoking is not permitted on the aircraft or in the airport. Thank you for your cooperation. We hope you've enjoyed your flight and we look forward to seeing you again very soon.'

The 747 taxied along the runway and rolled to a stop alongside the terminal.

Inside the plane, the seatbelt sign was switched off and passengers stood up to retrieve their hand baggage.

Outside the plane, a long flat-bedded truck parked beside the luggage compartment. A man in fluorescent overalls muttered into a walkie-talkie. His colleague pressed a button and turned a lever, opening the door in the side of the plane. The two men moved quickly and efficiently, pulling bags and suitcases out of the luggage compartment and onto the truck. They had been working for three minutes when one of the men muttered, 'I don't believe it.'

'What's happened?' asked the other.

'Some idiot didn't close his bag properly.'

A pair of socks, a shirt, a book and a few other items had come loose and rolled across the luggage compartment. The baggage handler grabbed them, stuffed them into the suitcase and slammed the lid. He tried to close the catches, but the zip seemed to have snapped. When that happens, there's only one thing to do. The baggage handler reached into his pocket, pulled out an orange strap, looped it around the suitcase and tied it with a knot. He passed the suitcase to his colleague, who added it to the pile on the truck.

There wasn't a cloud in the sky. The sun beat down on Kingsford Smith Airport, coating the plane, the passengers and their luggage with a blistering heat.

The warmth brought Grk back to life.

He hadn't actually been dead, of course. He'd just been so dazed by the cold that his body had shut down, conserving its energy, keeping him alive by sending him into a deep sleep. Now his eyes snapped open and his limbs wriggled and he tried to work out where he was.

Grk didn't know that he'd travelled halfway around the world. He simply thought that he'd been locked inside a cold, dark space for a long, long time. As far as he knew, he was right where he started, a short sprint from Cuddles Kennels. The temperature had changed. Some smells were different. But Trevor Cuddle was probably just around the corner, carrying a bucket in each hand. His family would be with him, laden with leashes and muzzles and walkie-talkies, determined to hunt down the dog who had eaten their lunch, escaped from their kennels and made them look like idiots.

Grk didn't want to see the Cuddles ever again but he needed to get out of this case. Determined to escape as fast as possible, he arched his back against one side of the suitcase, pressed his four paws against the other and pushed with all his strength.

Chapter 12

When the luggage compartment was empty, the two baggage handlers boarded their truck and drove quickly to the terminal.

They were listening to the radio at full volume, nodding their heads and tapping their feet in time to a tune. Neither of them gave the bags another glance. Which was why neither of them had noticed that one of the suitcases was wobbling back and forth as though it had suddenly come alive.

They parked their truck beside the terminal and unloaded the luggage onto a revolving carousel. Piece by piece, the baggage was whisked through a curtain...

... and into the terminal...

... where four hundred and sixteen passengers awaited the arrival of their possessions. A few minutes from now, they would be riding buses and taxis to their homes and hotels. They just had to wait for their luggage. But where was it?

There! The first bag appeared on the carousel.

A lucky passenger darted forwards, grabbed his suitcase and headed towards the exit, delighted to be the first to escape.

Other passengers pressed forwards, watching the stream of suitcases on the carousel, waiting for theirs.

'Cripes,' said a short man in a blue suit. 'What's that?'

He pointed at a suitcase that was bouncing from side to side, threatening to leap off the carousel.

'It's a bomb!' yelled his wife. 'Call the cops!'

The man in the blue suit reached for his phone. But before he or anyone else could do anything, there was a loud SNAP as the orange cord broke in half. The suitcase fell open like a book, spilling shirts, skirts, socks, blouses, books and a small white dog whose half-frozen limbs stuck out at strange angles.

Some of the passengers jumped backwards, trying to escape, and the others hustled forwards, hoping for a better view.

'It's alive!' shouted the man in a blue suit.

'It's got teeth!' yelled his wife.

'That's my bag!' shrieked a woman who had suddenly recognised not just her own suitcase, but a cotton skirt decorated with tiny pink flowers, which she had bought last week in Selfridges. She'd been looking forward to wearing it in Sydney. She hadn't expected to see it draped around the shoulders of a small white dog. She ran forwards with both arms extended and yelled, 'Give back my skirt!'

Grk was dazed, confused and not entirely thawed, but he could still summon the energy to roll over, wriggle out of her grasp and hobble along the luggage belt, trailing the skirt behind him.

People screamed and yelled and reached for their cameras, wanting to snap a picture of this strange creat-ure, a frozen monster in a flowery dress.

The luggage belt was like an assault course. Grk

43

scrambled over suitcases, bounced over a buggy, slid down a surfboard, skidded on a rucksack and slammed onto the floor.

'Stop him!' shouted the skirt's owner. 'Someone, please, stop that dog!'

Several people sprang forwards.

Grk could see a forest of hands reaching for him. He could hear voices shouting at him, ordering him to 'SIT!' or 'STAY!'

Some dogs would have cowered in terror. Others would have squatted obediently on the floor and waited for their masters to come and fetch them.

Grk just ran.

He didn't know where he was going. All he knew was this: a hundred crazy people were chasing him, shouting and screaming and waving their arms, and he didn't want to be caught by any of them.

Someone lunged for the skirt and grabbed a handful of flowery cotton. For a moment, Grk froze. Then he tugged himself free. There was a loud

riiiiiiiiiiiiiiiiiiiiiip . . .

. . . and the skirt tore in half.

A sobbing wail echoed through the airport. 'My skirt! My beautiful skirt! What have you done to it, you horrible dog?'

Even if he'd wanted to, Grk couldn't have answered that question. And he definitely didn't want to. He ducked under a table, scampered between a woman's legs and sprinted down a long white corridor marked NOTHING TO DECLARE.

Airports are always prepared for emergencies. Employees know how to behave if there is a fire, a bomb, an accident – or an escaped animal.

Customs officials and passport inspectors chattered on their walkie-talkies. Shutters slid down to cover the windows of expensive boutiques. Alarms buzzed. Armed guards blocked every door of the VIP lounge. Cameras swivelled. In the control room, lights flashed and a man in a dark-grey uniform spoke a stream of code words into a telephone: 'Alpha, Zero, Charlie, Foxtrot, Dingo, Six. I repeat: Alpha, Zero, Charlie, Foxtrot, Dingo, Six.'

'Understood,' said a voice on the end of the line.

Alpha, Zero, Charlie, Foxtrot, Dingo, Six was a secret code devised by the security staff. Anyone who understood the code would now know that there was a dog running wild.

Three minutes later, a blue van marked with the words DOG UNIT screeched to a halt outside the airport.

The doors swung open. Four bulky men sprang out of the van, wearing white overalls and carrying rifles loaded with tranquiliser darts. They charged through the door marked ARRIVALS.

Chapter 13

Shane glanced at his watch.

If his next client arrived on time, the flight would leave in precisely thirty minutes. Before then, he had to check the engine and prepare his route. He'd better get going. Shane quickened his pace and hurried across the tarmac, heading for his helicopter.

The helicopter wasn't actually *his*, of course. It belonged to Botany Bay Air Taxis, the company that paid his wages.

BBAT rented helicopters to rich business people who had an allergy to traffic jams. For a few hundred dollars, you could have your own helicopter for the day – and your own pilot too.

Thirty minutes from now, a wealthy businesswoman named Mrs Patricia White would climb aboard the helicopter. Shane would fly her and her personal assistant to a helipad on the roof of a skyscraper in the business district. He would wait there until Mrs White had finished her meeting or her dinner or her shopping or whatever she was doing, then bring her back to the airport for her flight to Adelaide.

It was easy work, the money was good and he got to fly a nice, shiny helicopter. What could be better than that?

Some pilots stepped aboard their helicopters only a minute or two in advance of their passengers, but Shane preferred to arrive at least half an hour early, giving himself enough time to make a few final checks of the engine and the rotors. If you're going to trust a machine with your life, you want to know that all its parts are working perfectly.

He walked briskly around the side of a long, low hangar. Several helicopters were parked in a row. All of them belonged to Botany Bay Air Taxis. At the end of the line, Shane could see his own machine, an orange Bell Jetranger with BBAT printed in large green letters on its side.

Then he saw the dog.

It was running towards him at great speed.

Shane wondered what it was doing here.

You didn't often see dogs running round airports. A guard dog, yes. Police dogs too. And some sniffer dogs hunting for drugs or explosives. But this dog didn't look like one of them. It looked like an ordinary pet that had lost its owner.

'Come here, doggie,' said Shane, clapping his hands to attract the dog's attention. 'Doggie! Nice doggie! Over here!'

The dog took no notice. It whizzed past Shane without a second glance, heading for the other end of the hangar.

'No worries,' said Shane, shrugging his shoulders. He wasn't offended. He was just about to turn his back and head for his helicopter when the dog suddenly skidded to a standstill.

Shane wondered what it was doing.

The dog turned round, its nose in the air, its nostrils twitching.

And trotted back to Shane, its tail wagging excitedly as if it had suddenly recognised the scent of an old friend.

Shane said, 'Hello, little doggie.'

The dog darted back and forth at Shane's feet as if he wanted to play a game.

'You want to be mates, do you? What's your name?'

The dog glanced at Shane for a second as if to say, *That's a really stupid question.* And then continued darting back and forth at his feet.

'I don't know what you want,' said Shane. 'What are you trying to tell me? You're hungry? You're thirsty? You're lost? Hey, there's a thought. Let's see who you are.'

He reached for the dog's collar.

The dog jumped backwards as if he'd suddenly decided that Shane wasn't such a nice bloke after all.

'Don't worry,' said Shane. 'I'm not going to hurt you. I'm just wondering who you are. I'm sure I've seen you somewhere before. Do you belong to one of the pilots?'

The dog wagged his tail. That might have meant 'yes'. But, just as easily, it might have meant 'no'.

Shane folded his arms over his chest and took a long look at the dog. Then he shook his head. 'No, I'd have remembered a nice little dog like yourself. It must have been somewhere else. Where was it? You're not Tony's, I know that much. He has a labrador. Kevin has that horrible poodle his ex-wife left behind. So where do I

48

know you from? You don't live in a pub, do you?'

The dog didn't answer. He just kept wagging his tail.

'Which one?' asked Shane. 'The Rocket? The Acropolis? The Rubber Chicken?'

The dog sat down, his tongue hanging out, his tail thumping on the tarmac.

Something about the way that the dog was sitting must have triggered a distant memory, because Shane suddenly remembered where he had seen this dog before. Or, rather, where he had seen a dog who looked just like this one, because there was no way that the two of them were the same animal.

'Oh, yes,' said Shane. 'That's right. You look like that little dog in the jungle. If I remember correctly, I saved his life. Now, what was he called? He had a strange name, I can remember that much. What was it? Geoff? No, no. Greg? No, something much stranger than that. Chuck? Muck? Brooke? Hook? Oh, that's it! I've got it! That dog was called Grk!'

Hearing his name, Grk sprang to his feet and wagged his tail with wild enthusiasm.

Shane stared at the little white dog in astonishment. 'You're not Grk, are you?'

Grk's little tail wagged so fast that he looked as if he might take off and fly around the airport.

Shane shook his head. 'Oh, come on, mate! Be serious! That's just not possible. I met Grk in Brazil and you're in Sydney. How could you have got from there to here? No, no, you're not Grk. You're just some other mutt who looks like him.'

Grk didn't answer. Of course he didn't. Dogs can't talk. But he gazed desperately into Shane's eyes, asking for his help.

You see Grk didn't recognise people by their faces, or their clothes, or their voices.

No, the only thing that mattered to Grk was *smell*.

And he was quite sure that he had smelled Shane before.

He was right, of course. He had met Shane in a small plane that crashed in the middle of a Brazilian jungle. There, Shane had saved his life, and Tim's too. If you want to know exactly what happened, you'd better read *Grk and the Pelotti Gang*.

Shane didn't have a very good sense of smell, so he couldn't tell that this little white dog was the same little white dog that he'd met in Brazil. In fact, he couldn't believe that it could possibly be the same animal. But then why would the dog answer to the name Grk?

Shane looked around the hangar. When he'd met Grk in Brazil, the little dog had been accompanied by two boys, one British and the other Brazilian. Could he remember their names? Oh, yes. That's right. They had been called Tim and Zito.

There was no sign of them.

Then that was that, thought Shane. This couldn't be the same dog. It just wasn't possible. Dogs don't travel between continents without their owners.

Pity.

He'd like to see those kids again. He left them without saying goodbye.

At the time, he didn't have any choice. He knew that

the police were on their way and he didn't want to stick around to say hello.

For some reason, the police didn't like Shane. They never said, 'Good afternoon, my old friend,' or 'How lovely to see you!'

No, they always greeted him with words like 'Put your hands in the air' or 'Don't you know this is private property?'

Shane preferred to keep his distance from the police. Over the years, they'd caused him a whole heap of bother. He couldn't understand why. He wasn't a criminal. Sure, he might have broken a few laws. But he wasn't a thief or a killer. He was just an ordinary man who needed to earn a living.

Right now, he was earning an honest wage, flying private helicopters for Botany Bay Air Taxis. The work wasn't exactly exciting, but it was a good way to earn some money. And legal too.

Work, thought Shane. That's right. That's what I'm meant to be doing. Preparing the chopper for Mrs Patricia White. Not standing around, dreaming about Brazil.

He looked at the dog. 'Still here, are you?'

The dog wagged his tail.

'You're welcome to stick around. But if we're going to be buddies, I'd like to know your name. Can I have a look at your collar?'

Without waiting for an answer, Shane leaned down and took hold of the dog's red collar.

This time, the dog didn't flinch. In fact, he licked Shane's hand.

'Stop it,' said Shane. 'That tickles.'

The dog licked him again.

'Don't do that, mate! Let me see your collar.'

The dog wriggled and squirmed, then licked him again.

'Hold still, mate. Stop moving. Please!' Shane grasped the red collar strapped around the dog's neck. There was a small silver tag attached to the collar. It was engraved with a string of numerals.

It didn't look like an Australian number. Nor Brazilian. Perhaps it was British.

Only one way to find out.

Shane pulled out his phone and dialled the number.

It rang four times. After the fourth ring, a voice said, 'Hello, this is the answerphone for Terence and Melanie Malt. Please leave a message after the tone and we'll call you back as soon as we can. If you'd like to leave a message for Tim, Max or Natascha, you can do that too. Thank you.'

Tim, thought Shane.

That was the kid's name.

It *is* his dog!

He spoke into the phone. 'G'day,' he said. 'This is a message for Tim. It's Shane here. We met in Brazil. I'm in Sydney right now and . . . Well, this probably sounds really strange, but have you lost your dog? Because I think I've found him.'

He left his number and asked Tim to call him.

Then he looked at the dog. 'What am I going to do with you, eh?'

The dog didn't answer. He just wagged his tail.

Chapter 14

In the morning, Tim was the first to get up.

The house was quiet. Mr and Mrs Malt were still asleep.

Tim tiptoed down the stairs, padding past his parents' closed door, taking great care to avoid the creaky floorboards. He glanced sadly at Grk's empty basket and went into the kitchen.

On an ordinary Monday morning, Tim would fix the lead to Grk's collar and take him for a walk around the block for fifteen minutes. Grk always seemed to find a new hedge to sniff or a fresh tree to pee on.

Today, there wouldn't be any walks. The local kerbs and lampposts held no interest for Tim. Instead, he fetched himself a glass of orange juice and sat at the computer. He found a good photo of Grk and attached it to a blank document. Then he typed slowly and quietly, not wanting to wake anyone else:

HAVE YOU SEEN OUR DOG?
His name is Grk.
He went missing on Sunday morning.
He was last seen outside Cuddles Kennels.
If you see him, please call us.
We miss him and we want him back!
WE WILL PAY A LARGE REWARD!!!!

At the bottom of the sheet, Tim put his mum and dad's mobile-phone numbers and their home number. He printed a single copy to make sure it looked good, then did ninety-nine more.

The printer was still spitting out sheets of paper when Mrs Malt came into the kitchen, rubbing her wet hair with a towel. She said, 'Good morning, Tim. You're up early. Are you finishing your homework?'

'I didn't have any.'

'Then what's that?'

'Nothing.'

'Let me see.'

'It's nothing,' said Tim, pulling the papers from the printer and folding them in half, hiding what was written on the front.

'It's obviously not nothing.' His mother held out her hand. 'Let me see.'

Tim reluctantly handed over the stack of sheets. Mrs Malt read the top copy, then flicked through the others to make sure they were the same. She fixed her son with a stern expression. 'What are you planning to do with these?'

'Nothing.'

'Tim, do you think I'm a complete fool?'

'No, Mum.'

'Then don't "nothing" me. I don't want to be "nothinged" ever again. Just tell the truth. What were you planning to do with them?'

Tim thought for a moment about lying, then realised that there was no point. She'd know he was fibbing. 'I'm going to go back to Cuddles Kennels and fix them to every tree and every lamppost. Someone must have seen Grk. If they bring him back, I'm going to give them all my pocket money as a reward.'

Mrs Malt sighed. 'I'm sorry, Tim. It's a sweet idea, but we can't go back there today.'

'Why not?'

'It's Monday.'

'So?'

'I have to go to work. Your father does too. And you have to go to school.'

'School?' cried Tim, shocked that his mother could even mention such a word. 'I can't go to school! Don't you understand what's happened? Grk is missing!'

'I know he is,' said Mrs Malt. 'We can look for him later. Right now, it's time for school.'

Tim couldn't believe it.

If this was a normal Monday, he'd go to school. He wouldn't want to, of course. But he'd go anyway. There are some things you just have to do. Life is like that.

But today was not a normal Monday. Today, Grk was lost. Today, Grk might be wandering through the fields and woods near Cuddles Kennels, hungry and thirsty, howling and whining, confused and desperate, trying to get home. Or he might have been kidnapped. Or he might have been injured. He might be lying in a ditch, his leg broken, crying and moaning, waiting for someone to help him.

Were they just going to abandon him?

Yes, they were. That was what Mrs Malt had decided, anyway. She insisted that Tim had to get ready for school as if nothing unusual had happened.

'Why can't I take the day off?' said Tim.

'Because you can't.'

'Why not?'

'Because I say so.'

'Don't you care about Grk?'

'Of course I do.'

'Then why can't I take the day off?'

'Because I say so,' said Mrs Malt. 'Now, have you had breakfast?'

'I'm not hungry.'

Actually, that wasn't true. He was starving. He sat down at the kitchen table and ate a bowl of Shreddies and two pieces of toast with strawberry jam. When his father came downstairs, Tim tried to talk to him about Grk, but Mr Malt said, 'Let's talk about it later. I've got a breakfast meeting and I mustn't be late.'

'But, Dad—'

'Not now,' said Mr Malt. He grabbed his briefcase, kissed his wife, waved to his son and rushed out of the house.

Fifteen minutes later, Tim and his mother left the house too. Mrs Malt was just closing the front door when she heard the sound of the phone ringing inside the house. She paused for a moment, then slammed the door.

Tim said, 'Don't you want to answer that?'

Mrs Malt shook her head. 'It won't be important.'

'How do you know?'

'If it's important, they'll ring my mobile. Come on, let's go. You don't want to be late for school, do you?'

'Yes, I do.'

Mrs Malt just smiled and ushered him towards the car.

Chapter 15

Shane liked having a dog around. Flying a helicopter can be a lonely business. You have passengers, of course. But they don't usually like to chat. They're flying by helicopter because they're exceedingly busy and astonishingly rich, so they prefer to spend any spare moments on the phone to their lawyer or their stockbroker, checking on the progress of their deals. They don't want to waste time talking to someone as unimportant as their pilot.

Grk didn't talk much either. But he was a good listener. As Shane checked the helicopter, making sure that the engineers had cleaned the engine and filled the tank to the brim, he chatted to Grk as if they were old friends. He explained that he had been travelling around the world for the past few years, but his experiences in South America had convinced him to come home again. He still wasn't sure if he'd made the right decision. Every time he came to work, he thought about jumping on a plane and flying to a different continent. He'd miss his mum and dad, of course. He saw more of them now. He described their small house in Wagga Wagga and their quiet, ordinary existence. He talked about his own little flat in Surry Hills and the lonely life that he had been leading since he returned to Sydney. He wondered if he was ever going to find a place where he really wanted to live or a woman who would be willing to share it with him.

'That's done,' said Shane, wiping oil from his hands. 'She's all ready to go.'

Just as those words left his mouth, the dog darted under the nearest helicopter and hid in the shadows. A moment later, a shout echoed across the tarmac. 'Hey! You!'

Shane was surprised to see two men running towards him, carrying rifles. He wondered if he should put his hands in the air. Were they crooks? Or police? As the two men came closer, he saw that they were wearing white overalls marked with the words DOG UNIT. When they reached him, one of the men asked, 'Have you seen a dog?'

'What sort of dog?' said Shane.

'A white one.'

Shane said, 'Did he have black patches? And a little tail which wouldn't stop wagging?'

'That's him,' said one of the men.

'Where is he?' said the other.

'Why are you asking?' said Shane. 'Is he yours?'

'He's a runaway, mate.'

'We think he arrived on a plane.'

'Could be highly dangerous.'

'Probably riddled with disease.'

'Rabies, most likely.'

'Fleas too.'

'You name it, mate, these dogs have the lot.'

'Where did he go?'

Shane pointed in the wrong direction. 'That way.'

'Thanks, mate,' said one of the men.

'Much obliged,' said the other.

Together, the two Dog Unit officers sprinted across the tarmac, clutching their rifles, and disappeared round the side of the hangar.

Shane wondered why he'd lied to them.

Because they were like dog police, perhaps. And he never liked helping the police.

There was another reason too. He liked that little dog. Whoever it was. He didn't want it to get locked up by the dog unit.

Shane leaned down and peered into the shadows under the helicopter.

'They've gone,' he whispered. 'You can come out now.'

But he was talking to himself.

The dog had disappeared.

Chapter 16

Grk didn't have a plan.

Like most dogs, he didn't make plans. In fact, he never thought about the future at all.

He only really worried about food and sleep and warmth. And worrying about them took up most of the spare space in his small brain.

His body had warmed up nicely, so he went for a little walk, stretching his limbs and exploring his new-found surroundings. He didn't wonder where he was going or what might happen when he got there. He just trotted around the hangars and across the runways, enjoying the sunshine and the warm air, stopping every now and then to have a pee against a wall or on a patch of tarmac.

Until he smelled food.

And not just any old food – one of his favourite foods on the entire planet. A treat to tempt the palate of the most discerning canine gourmet. Not far from here, his sensitive nostrils could definitely sense the delectable scent of a chicken pie.

Mmmmmmm. That was a good smell. A chicken pie with gloopy gravy and flaky pastry and plump chunks of chicken. Exactly what was needed to fill the empty stomach of a hungry young dog.

Grk's stomach was very, very empty. It was a long

time since those sausages. All he wanted was some good food.

A chicken pie, for instance.

All his senses drove him onwards, searching for the source of that adorable smell. He ran across the runway until he reached a large black van. The smell was coming from inside. And the door was open. Grk didn't hesitate. He sprang inside. And there, lying on the driver's seat, he found what he was looking for.

A half-eaten chicken pie. Still wrapped in its paper bag.

Grk stared at the pie for a few seconds, thinking through his options.

He had stolen things before. Food, usually. Tennis balls too. And the odd sock. He knew what happened if someone caught him. They shouted and threw their arms around and sometimes even tried to kick him.

He didn't want to be kicked.

But the pie smelled so good...

He couldn't resist it. He clamped his jaws into the pastry and started eating.

He had only taken a single mouthful – and hadn't even swallowed it properly – when he heard voices.

They were getting louder. Coming closer.

Grk looked at the pie.

What should he do? Run? Hide? Or keep eating?

The answer was obvious.

Holding the pie very carefully in his jaws, he squeezed between the seats and sneaked into the back of the van.

A moment later, two men clambered into the front of the van. They were wearing paint-splattered dungarees. The driver put the keys in the ignition, then said, 'Where's my pie, mate?'

'What pie?' said his passenger.

'I was eating a chicken pie. It's disappeared.'

'Where did you leave it?'

'On this seat.'

'Then you're probably sitting on it.'

'I'm not, mate. I'd know if I was sitting on a pie.'

'Maybe you lost it.'

'Maybe you stole it.'

'Oh, come on, mate. Do you really think I'd steal your pie?'

'You might.'

'I wouldn't.'

'Then where is it?'

'I don't know, mate. Maybe you ate it.'

'I'm not an idiot. I'd remember eating a pie.'

'This is ridiculous, mate. Are we going to sit here all night talking about your pie? Or are we going to have a beer?'

'Let's have a beer.' The driver turned the key in the ignition and started the engine.

In the back of the van, Grk was eating the most delicious pie on the planet.

Over the years, he had eaten several succulent steaks, some mouthwatering cakes, all kinds of interesting cheeses and a whole host of other fine foods, but he had never tasted anything as perfectly flaky and majestically gloopy as this particular chicken pie.

He heard the doors slamming and the men talking and the engine starting. He felt the van lurching forwards. But he took no notice. All his attention was concentrated on the pie. He dug his teeth through the soft pastry and bit into a moist cube of chicken.

When Grk finally finished his meal, he sat up and looked around. His nostrils twitched. He could smell the last lingering traces of the chicken, mingling with other older, mouldier scents. He wondered what else might be hidden in the van.

Time to explore!

He wandered through the back of the van, poking his nose down every hole and into every crevice.

He quickly unearthed a little trove of treasures. A mouldy apple with one bite taken out of it. A square of chocolate. Some salt and vinegar crisps. A half-eaten Vegemite sandwich. Yum! Yum! Yummity-yum! He ate everything except the apple. (Grk didn't care for fruit.) Then he licked his lips, walked three times in a circle, lay down, closed his eyes and went to sleep.

Chapter 17

When they got to school, Mrs Malt had a word with Tim's headmaster, asking if the teachers could keep an eye on Tim throughout the day.

'You know what he's like,' she said, ruffling her son's hair. 'Leave him alone for a moment and he'll jump on a plane to Brazil or catch a train to Paris. Please don't let that happen. We've already lost our dog. We don't want to lose our son too.'

'You don't have to worry,' said the headmaster. 'Tim will be perfectly safe here.'

Tim didn't like the sound of that.

He knew what 'perfectly safe' meant.

It meant he would be watched all day. His teachers would never let him out of their sight. He wouldn't be allowed to wander off or sneak away. They'd keep a careful eye on him.

He didn't want them to watch him at all.

He wanted to be free.

Chapter 18

Grk sat up. He'd heard a worrying noise. A loud rattle. Followed by a clunk, a bang and a creak.

He understood what was happening. Someone was opening the back of the van. They wanted their pie back.

But they were going to be disappointed. Their pie had gone. It was buried at the bottom of his stomach and it wasn't coming out again.

When the pie's owners discovered this unfortunate fact, what would they do?

They would probably kick him. They would definitely shout at him. And they might well lock him in a deep, dark dungeon for the rest of his days.

They could only do all this, of course, if they caught him.

He would have to be faster than them. And more cunning too. He would have to wriggle out of their grasp and run and run and run until he was a long, long way away from here.

He crouched in the back of the van, waiting and listening, preparing himself for the perfect moment.

He was surrounded by ladders and toolboxes covered in thick woollen blankets, but he didn't bother investigating them. His sensitive nose had already told him that they didn't contain food, and nothing apart from food would have interested him. He simply crouched on the floor, his muscles tensed, and listened to the rattling, the clunking and the bangs.

A door swung open. Light swarmed into the back of the van.

This was his moment – his one chance.

Grk sprang forwards.

He catapulted through the open doors, bounced off one man and landed on another.

For a moment, the two men were too surprised to speak. Then they both spoke at once.

One of them said, 'Wha—?'

The other said, 'Jeez!'

The two men lunged forwards with outstretched arms – and knocked their heads together.

'Uh!' cried one, clutching his chin.

'Ow!' cried the other, holding his forehead.

Grk had already gone. As soon as his paws touched the ground, he started running and now he was dodging between two oncoming cars in the middle of the road.

The two men stared after him. Then they looked at one another.

'Was that a dog?' said one, clutching his forehead.

'It certainly looked like a dog,' said the other, rubbing his chin.

'What was it doing in my van?'

'I'll tell you exactly what it was doing, mate. Eating your chicken pie.'

Grk sprinted across the road, ignoring the cars, which tooted their horns at him, and sped down the pavement.

He wanted to put as much distance as possible between him and the two men.

He ran for a minute or two, then paused and looked behind him.

There was no sign of the chicken pie's owners or their van. They weren't following him. He had escaped.

Grk lifted his head and sniffed the air, wondering what to do next. Where should he go?

How about some food?

That was a good idea.

The chicken pie, which had filled his stomach so comfortably, had now been digested and there was an empty space in Grk's belly, waiting to be filled.

He sniffed the air once more.

He could smell salt and diesel and trees and sewage and people and other dogs and cats and rats and rope and rubbish and food.

Food!

What type of food?

He wasn't sure. The source of the smell wasn't very close. He might have to go a long way. But he was sure that the effort would be worthwhile.

He started walking.

Chapter 19

Outside Sydney Opera House, a large crowd had gathered. All of them were dressed in their finest clothes. Beautiful women glittered with expensive jewellery and sleek men showed off their tans and their Rolexes.

Many of the richest and most important people in Sydney were here tonight. Bankers and brokers, restaurant owners and wine makers, shipping magnates, ambassadors, the owner of a TV station, a man who controlled half the copper mines in Asia, a woman whose supermarkets supplied half the homes in Australia – all of them headed into the main entrance of the Opera House.

The performance would be starting soon. No one wanted to be late.

Tonight, the Opera House was hosting an exclusive event, a special performance of *Fidelio*, Beethoven's only opera.

The cheapest tickets cost two hundred dollars and the most expensive were two thousand. All profits went to charity.

The audience comprised of many of the richest people in Sydney. Some loved opera. Some hated opera, but loved spending time with other rich people. All of them were looking forward to the night ahead.

They were sure it would be a night to remember.

*

The world doesn't have many sights more beautiful than the Harbour Bridge, the colossal steel structure that joins the north and south sides of Sydney, but Grk didn't even notice it. He trotted along Circular Quay, ignoring the glorious sights that surrounded him, and headed for the source of the smell. As he got closer, the smells grew clearer, and he walked faster. Oh, yes. Yum, yum. That smelled good. Meaty things and fishy things and spicy things too. His sensitive nose distinguished caviar and smoked salmon and chips and cheese and salami and several other smells that he couldn't recognise but wanted to explore. Saliva collected around his tongue and dribbled out of his mouth. His head held high, he trotted down a flight of stairs and emerged in a small loading area at the back of the Opera House.

He saw a white van. The doors were open. Men in neat uniforms were removing trays from the back of the van and carrying them through a doorway.

There was a reception after the opera. The audience, the orchestra, the singers and the conductor would mingle together, shaking hands and making conversation, drinking champagne and eating canapés.

Here they were.

Tray after tray after tray of elegant little snacks.

Just waiting to be eaten.

Grk wasn't a bad dog.

If he'd been with Tim or Max or Natascha, he wouldn't have gone anywhere near the white van. He would have trotted away, following his owners, confident that they would provide him with a decent meal as soon as they got home.

But he was alone.

So he had to look after himself.

And he was hungry.

His empty stomach had been sending a series of signals to his brain, begging for food, and Grk wasn't the type of dog who ignored his stomach. Especially since the signals had been getting louder and louder as he came closer and closer to the source of these delectable smells.

Grk watched the waiters as they hurried to and fro, taking trays from the back of the van, and picked his moment perfectly. When their backs were turned, he darted forwards, jumped into the van and buried his nose in a tray of spicy spring rolls.

Ah! The smell! And, even better, the taste!

Grk gulped down a mouthful, and was just about to gulp down another, when his attention was distracted by another even more delicious scent, wafting towards him from the other side of the van.

He turned round, sprang and sampled a tray of cheese, then grabbed several slices of salami and swallowed them down, freeing his mouth for more treats.

He had never been so happy.

Surrounded by such a feast, he hardly knew which way to turn, so he simply tried to stuff his mouth as full as possible with as many different snacks as he could fit between his jaws. He gulped and chomped and chewed and grabbed and gulped and—

'Hey! What do you think you're doing? Get out of there!'

A furious red-faced waiter shook his fist at Grk. Then he hauled himself into the van and lurched forwards with his arms raised.

Grk was a polite and sociable dog. He liked meeting new people. But sometimes he preferred his own company. He took a final sausage roll, sprang out of the van, dodged past the waiter and sprinted across the tarmac.

The waiter jumped out of the van and shouted at the top of his voice, summoning reinforcements.

People came from all directions.

Grk ran round the Opera House, pursued by shouts and footsteps. He charged up some stairs and across a plaza and down some more stairs.

Ahead, he could see a large crowd of people. Women in long dresses. Men in dinner jackets and bow ties. They saw him too. Some shouted. Others screamed. One held out his arms and yelled, 'Here, doggy! Come here, doggy! Nice doggy!'

Grk wasn't that stupid. He took no notice of the yelling man or anyone else. He just ran through the crowd at full speed, leaving a trail of smashed glasses and angry waiters and confused security guards and a tourist with a camera who recorded the whole thing and later sold the film for enough money to extend his holiday for an entire week.

Grk was quicker than any of them. He dodged out of their way, avoiding their hands and their legs, ran down a flight of stairs, sprang through an open doorway and disappeared into the depths of the Opera House. People pounded after him. Grk could hear their footsteps. He sped along corridor after corridor till he came to a storage room stacked with forty or fifty large wooden crates, used for carrying scenery from one theatre to another, and that was where he decided to stop. Grk darted behind the nearest crate, threw himself to the floor and waited to see if he was being followed.

A minute passed. Then another. He couldn't hear any footsteps. His pursuers must have lost him. They had given up or gone the wrong way.

He was safe.

He picked himself up and explored his new home. He soon found a mouldy old blanket that stank of socks.

He licked the last crumbs of cheese from his lips, then lay down and rolled over, wrapping the blanket around himself.

Grk had a short memory.

A couple of minutes ago, he had been running up stairs and through corridors, terrified by the mad horde of angry people just an arm's length behind him.

But now, a couple of minutes later, he had forgotten all about them. In fact, he couldn't have been happier.

His stomach was full. The blanket was warm and cosy. The smell reminded him of the laundry basket at home, which was one of his favourite places for a mid-afternoon nap.

He soon drifted into a deep, comfortable sleep.

Chapter 20

That day, Tim felt like a prisoner. The classroom was his cell and the teachers were his wardens. Even when he went to the loo, one of them stood outside the door, waiting for him to emerge.

They weren't taking any chances.

He wished he could tell them that they were making a big mistake.

Don't worry, he wanted to say. You don't have to watch me all the time. I'm not going to run away. Grk's a clever little dog and he can look after himself. Wherever he is and whatever he might be doing, he's going to be fine. He doesn't need my help – and I wouldn't want to help him even if I could.

But if he *had* said all that to his teachers, he would have been lying. In actual fact, he was desperate to escape from his stupid school and join the search for Grk. It was all he wanted to do.

If his teachers hadn't been watching him, he would have slipped out of the door, sprinted across the yard, dodged through the gates and found his own way back to Cuddles Kennels.

Trevor Cuddle and his family had promised to devote all their spare time to the search, but Tim didn't trust them. Much more likely, he thought, they would be looking after the other dogs in their kennels and forgetting all about Grk. To them, Grk was just one more dog, no more or less interesting than any of the others in their care.

Tim felt very differently. To him, there was nothing in the world more important than Grk. That was why he wanted to be there himself, hunting through the countryside, shouting, 'Grk! Grk! Where are you, Grk?'

Mrs Malt had confiscated his posters, but she'd probably just put them in her desk. If not, he could print a hundred more.

As soon as he got home, he decided, he would assemble whatever he needed. He would take some tape and pins for the posters. Then he would select a few warm clothes, an anorak, a torch, a penknife and his pocket money. He'd hide everything under his bed. That night, he'd act perfectly normally. He'd do his homework and eat his supper and go to bed, pretending to his mum and dad that he'd forgotten all about Grk. He would wait till midnight. When his parents were asleep, he would sneak out of the house and head for Cuddles Kennels.

Once he got there, he would spend the rest of the night pinning posters to trees and wrapping them around lampposts.

With any luck, he'd be home again before dawn and no one would even suspect that he'd left the house.

Chapter 21

Grk was woken by a voice.

He sat up, immediately alert, his ears upright, and listened.

A second voice joined the first.

They were nearby.

Grk trotted down to the end of the crate, poked his nose round the corner and had a look at the men who were talking.

He had never smelled them before. They weren't the men and women who had been chasing him earlier. No, these were entirely new strangers.

They were talking in low voices as if they didn't want to be overheard.

They were dressed identically in black jeans and black shirts. They had heavy steel-tipped boots on their feet, black leather gloves covering their hands and black woollen caps perched on the back of their heads.

One of the men took a phone from his pocket and made a call.

A minute later, he was joined by two more men. Then three others. And yet more, until there were about twenty men standing around in a huddle, talking in low voices. All of them were dressed identically in black shirts, black jeans, black gloves, black caps and heavy steel-tipped boots.

Grk stayed behind the crate and watched them.

His nostrils twitched.

He could smell something good. He wasn't sure what it might be, but he knew he wanted to eat it.

He turned his head from side to side, searching for the source of the smell.

Sniff, sniff.

Sniff, sniff.

Ah! Yes! There it was!

On the other side of the crate, Grk could see an enormously fat man with a bright-red face. In one of his huge hands, the fat man was holding a packet of chocolate-coated hazelnuts. Every few moments, he dipped the chubby fingers of his other hand into the packet, pulled out a nut and popped it into his mouth.

Have you ever tasted a chocolate-coated hazelnut?

If you have, then I'm sure you'll agree that there are few things in the world more delicious.

Grk stared longingly at the packet, wondering how he was going to get the nuts out of the red-faced man's hands and into his own mouth.

The men worked in silence. No one asked any questions. They knew exactly what they were doing. Two of them opened a crate and reached inside. They passed guns, ammunition and explosives into the waiting hands of their companions. When the crate was empty, they opened another and emptied that too.

They looked like a well-trained band of soldiers, preparing for a fierce mission.

They took their orders from the red-faced man.

Actually, he didn't just have a red face. He had red hands too, and a red neck. If he had removed all his clothes, you would have seen that his enormously fat body was bright red from the very top of his round bald head to the very tip of his tiniest toe.

His name was Red Jelly and he was one of the most famous criminals in Australia. He had spent half his life in prison and the other half on the run from the police, stealing and spending and stealing some more. And now he was going to commit the biggest crime of his life.

Let me tell you how Red Jelly got his name.

It's very simple. And very horrible.

He was stung by a box jellyfish.

Have you heard of the box jellyfish?

No?

You've heard of jellyfish, haven't you? Those funny, wobbly creatures that shimmer through the sea, letting their tendrils drift in the water. If you bump into one of them while you're swimming, it might sting you, and you'll get a red rash.

If you bump into a box jellyfish, it will sting you so badly that you'll almost certainly be dead within four minutes.

Box jellyfish are among the most deadly creatures in existence. Very few people have ever survived an encounter with one of them. Which is why many Australian beaches are protected by safety nets, providing a jellyfish-free area where people can swim.

A box jellyfish has twenty-four eyes. It also has sixty long tentacles that trail through the water. Each one of the tentacles is filled with thousands of tiny poisonous darts.

If you are swimming in the sea and you suddenly realise that you are unlucky enough to be sharing a patch of water with a box jellyfish, get out!

Otherwise its tentacles will envelop your body. Hundreds of tiny darts will puncture your skin. Each one will deliver a brutal dose of poison. And, three or four minutes later, you will probably be dead.

Red Jelly was very lucky.

He went swimming in the ocean and was stung all over by a box jellyfish. His limbs swelled up. His skin turned bright red. He suffered appalling agony in every part of his body. He stayed in hospital for several months, recovering from his wounds.

But he didn't die.

When he came out of hospital, he looked like an enormous red blob of jelly. Someone said so, anyway. And the name stuck.

When the crates had been emptied and everything had been prepared, Red Jelly looked at his gang and spoke in a low voice: 'This is the big one, boys. This is the day we've been waiting for. Are you ready?'

'Yes, boss.' His men nodded. There were no jokes, no smiles. In the next few minutes, they would be risking their lives. A few hours from now, they might be dead. They might be in prison. Or they might be rich.

'Then let's go and make some money,' said Red Jelly.

He grabbed a handful of chocolate-coated hazelnuts and tossed them into his mouth. One of the hazelnuts fell to the floor, but he didn't bother picking it up. He just gulped down the others, turned himself round and headed towards a flight of stairs that led up towards the main stage of the Opera House. His men hurried after him, carrying guns and grenades and boxes of explosives.

None of them even glanced behind them. Which was why none of them noticed that they were being followed.

Grk sprang forwards, planted his paws on the floor, grabbed the hazelnut and gulped it down.

It was delicious.

But tiny.

Having eaten it, he seemed to feel even hungrier. The chicken pie was long-forgotten. Now, his stomach felt as empty as a desert. He wanted more hazelnuts. He *needed* more hazelnuts. Delicious crunchy hazelnuts smothered in sweet milk chocolate. He could taste them in his mouth. He could feel them crackling between his teeth. If he didn't get another one soon, he would probably go completely crazy.

Grk's tummy gurgled. Saliva dribbled from his jaws. He wanted a hundred more chocolate-coated hazelnuts and he would be prepared to do just about anything to get them.

He stayed in the shadows, hiding behind crates and big slabs of scenery, never allowing himself to be seen, but never letting Red Jelly or his gang out of his sight.

Chapter 22

The applause seemed to go on for ever. Cheers and whistles echoed around the auditorium. Shouts came from every corner:

'Bravo! Bravo!'

'Encore! Encore!'

The singers were standing in a line at the front of the stage, clutching bouquets and waving to their admirers. They stepped forwards and gave a final bow. Then the conductor nodded to the stage manager and the curtain was lowered for the last time.

The singers hurried to their dressing rooms, the orchestra filed out and the lights came on. It had been a triumphant performance of *Fidelio*, witnessed by an exclusive audience of the smartest folk in Sydney, paying premium prices for their tickets. Now a hubbub of happy chatter filled the Opera House as people rose to their feet and headed for the exits.

A loud BANG stopped them in their tracks.

No one knew what had happened. They looked around, wondering whether the scenery had exploded or a member of the orchestra had stumbled and smacked his foot into a kettledrum.

As they looked around the auditorium, their eyes were drawn irresistibly to a huge figure who had stepped through the heavy curtains and was now standing at the front of the stage. Opera singers are often enormous and many of tonight's performers had been vast, but this man was bigger than any of them. He was wearing a black shirt that bulged around his vast belly and his red skin glowed in the lights. From a distance, you might have mistaken him for the biggest tomato on the planet. His right hand was raised and he was pointing a pistol at the ceiling. He pulled the trigger. Another BANG filled the theatre.

The bullet smacked into the ceiling, releasing a handful of plaster, which fluttered gently over the audience like a sudden shower of snow.

No one moved. No one spoke. The entire audience remained rooted to the spot, watching the man on the stage, waiting to see what he would do next. Some people thought that he was part of the show, an additional extra performed by the opera company to entertain their admiring audience. Others wondered if he was a practical joker. But a few of them recognised him and felt a sudden jolt of panic, wondering why such a notorious criminal should have come to the opera.

Red Jelly took another step forwards and stood on the edge of the stage. He smiled. He didn't often have the attention of so many people, and it felt good. Then his deep voice boomed around the auditorium.

'Good evening,' he said. 'I hope you've all enjoyed yourselves.'

Red Jelly was wearing a microphone clipped to his shirt and his voice echoed from speakers all around the vast hall.

He smiled as if he was the host of a magnificent party and all these people were his guests. Then he reached into his pocket, pulled out a chocolate-coated hazelnut and popped it in his mouth. The microphone amplified the sound of his chewing.

CRACK!

CRUNCH!

GULP!

Red Jelly swallowed the last dregs of chocolate, then smiled once more. 'The bar is open,' he said. 'They'll be serving cold beer right now. I bet you want to go and have one. You've certainly deserved it, sitting through that whole long opera. But you're going to have to wait a little longer, my friends. This is now a siege and you are all my hostages.'

For a second, no one moved and no one spoke. Then panic-filled screams echoed around the auditorium. A few people fainted. Many more pulled out their phones and called the police. Several hundred men and woman surged in different directions, heading towards the nearest exit, trying to get away from the terrifying figure at the front of the stage ...

... but they immediately discovered that their escape routes were blocked. The doors were closed and armed guards in black uniforms prevented anyone from coming in or going out.

Red Jelly raised his gun again. He reached into his pocket, grabbed a couple of hazelnuts and tossed them into his mouth. They CRACKED and CRUNCHED again inside his mouth, then he GULPED them down and said in a quiet voice, 'Let me give you a piece of advice.'

The audience fell silent. No one wanted to be shot. Everyone faced forwards and waited to hear what the fat man was going to say.

'Don't bother running,' said Red Jelly, chomping nuts as he spoke. 'Don't bother fighting either. My men are armed with guns, but they have another weapon too. We have laid explosives throughout this opera house and the trigger is right here.' He patted his pocket. 'If I press this button, all of us – you and me and everyone else in here – we will all be blown to pieces. So, my friends, I suggest you keep calm, keep quiet and listen very carefully.'

Chapter 23

On an ordinary Monday night, the staff of the Sydney
Emergency Services Call Centre receive three or four
calls from idiots and jokers. They are the type of people
who don't seem to be worried about wasting valuable
police time. Tonight, for instance, one man rang to
complain that he had lost a sock down the back of the
sofa and asked if the fire brigade would be able to help
him find it. Another asked for directions from Tumba-
long Park to Central Station. A third claimed that a fat
man had taken three thousand people hostage at the
Sydney Opera House and was threatening to blow them
into a million pieces.

The Emergency Services did what they always did.
They listened carefully and sympathetically to whatever
the caller said. They noted down all the relevant details
and asked appropriate questions. And they promised to
investigate.

When you work for the Sydney Emergency Services
Call Centre, you know that even idiots and jokers have
to be taken seriously. Sometimes, they might be trying
to tell you something important.

A few moments later, a second caller rang the Sydney
Emergency Services Call Centre and made the same
claim that he was being held hostage in the Opera House
by a fat, red-faced man with a gun.

A moment after that, yet another caller said the same thing. And then another. And another. Followed by a hundred and fifty-three more. The lines jammed. The operators couldn't keep up. The Sydney Emergency Services Call Centre was overwhelmed by callers claiming to be hostages inside the Opera House. All of them said that their captor was an enormously fat man with a bright-red face, who was going to blow them up.

Were they all pranksters? Had they ganged together to play some kind of massive practical joke? Or were they telling the truth?

There was only one way to find out.

A message went to the Sydney Police, asking them to send an officer to the Opera House and investigate reports of a robbery or a siege.

Constable Bruce McDougall and Constable Bobby Kordellos had been strolling around Circular Quay, keeping an eye on the commuters heading back to Manly, making sure no one was drunk or disorderly. When they heard the message on their radios, they radioed back to say that they would check it out immediately. Then they started running.

Three minutes and forty-seven seconds later, Constables McDougall and Kordellos were running up the stairs and rushing through the main entrance of the Opera House, heading for the auditorium, determined to discover what was happening inside.

They reached the main door.

A carefully handwritten notice had been pinned to it.

THE OPERA HOUSE IS NOW CLOSED
ROBBERY IN PROGRESS
DO NOT ENTER OR HOSTAGES WILL BE KILLED
SIGNED: THE RED JELLY GANG

Constable McDougall tried to open the door. It was locked. He rattled the handle, then pulled out his gun and looked at his colleague. 'What do you think?'

'Might be a joke,' said Constable Kordellos.

'Might be, mate. Or might not.'

'Let's call it in.'

They retreated a few paces. Constable McDougall kept his gun trained on the door, while Constable Kordellos pulled out his radio and called the station. He explained what had happened and asked for instructions.

Chief Inspector Sam Somerville was lying on the sofa, twiddling his moustache and reading the latest issue of *Yacht Monthly*.

The kids were asleep. His wife had gone to bed for an early night. But Sam Somerville wanted to spend an hour or two poring over the small ads at the back of the magazine, checking out the photos and comparing prices. He was planning to buy a new boat.

At the weekends, Chief Inspector Somerville went sailing around Sydney Harbour in his little dinghy. His three sons went with him. They were getting bigger now and the boat was too small for them. It was time to buy a boat that all four of them would fit in. (Mrs Somerville didn't like sailing. The waves made her feel sick.)

If they bought a new yacht, they could head off together on a real voyage. Round the coast to Melbourne, maybe. Or even as far as New Zealand. Looking at the photos in the small ads column, Chief Inspector imagined himself and his three sons heading across the ocean, the sun warming their faces, the breeze blowing through their hair, the boat plunging through the waves. What could be better than that?

The phone rang.

The Chief Inspector picked up. In a quiet voice, not wanting to wake anyone else in the house, he said, 'Somerville speaking.'

One of his junior officers explained what was happening. Sam Somerville listened for two minutes. He asked three questions. Then he said, 'I'll be there as soon as I can.' He switched off the phone and sprang up from the sofa. He grabbed his car keys, ran upstairs, woke his wife and explained what was happening.

'Be careful,' she said.

'I'm always careful,' said Chief Inspector Somerville.

He kissed her goodbye. Then he hurried out of the house, got in the car and drove to Police Headquarters.

As he sped through the streets, he couldn't help smiling to himself.

He was worried about the hostages. Of course he was. He was worried about his men and women too, the men and women who would have to risk their lives to stop Red Jelly.

But he was also delighted.

Chief Inspector Somerville knew all about Red Jelly. He had put him in prison four times. Once for burglary, twice for armed robbery and once for escaping from prison in the middle of his sentence.

Six months ago, Red Jelly escaped again. Since then, Chief Inspector Somerville had been waiting for the call.

Now, finally, he was going to get a chance to put Red Jelly back where he belonged.

Chapter 24

Grk couldn't wait any longer.

He'd been standing in the wings for ages, waiting for his cue. He had been peering through the thick curtains, watching what was happening on stage. He'd seen the fat man shouting at the audience. He had witnessed panic and pandemonium.

During all this time, he had waited for the perfect moment.

But the perfect moment never came. And now he couldn't wait any longer.

He pushed aside the curtain and stepped onto the wooden stage.

A thousand unexpected smells swept into his nose, but he ignored all of them. He wasn't interested in the men and women crammed into the auditorium. No, all his attention was focused on one man, Red Jelly, and the packet of chocolate-coated hazelnuts in his pocket.

Grk walked across the stage. He approached the fat man. And he barked.

Woof!

The fat man took no notice. Perhaps he was deaf. Or perhaps he was a selfish pig who wanted to keep all the nuts for himself.

Only one way to find out.

Grk barked again, louder.

Woof! Woof!

This time, the fat man turned to look at him.

So did three thousand people.

They stared at Grk in silence and astonishment. A little white dog, in the middle of the stage of the most famous opera house on the planet, barking at an enormous, notorious and thoroughly wicked criminal. What did he think he was doing?

Grk knew exactly what he was doing. He was barking loudly to attract a fat man's attention. Now he did it again.

Woof! Woof! Woof!

He lay down and waggled his paws in the air. Then he sprang to his feet, sat up in a 'begging' position, put his head on one side and let his tongue hang out of his mouth. He looked pathetic, silly and very cute.

Red Jelly stared at the little dog.

He could have shooed him away. Or shouted at him. If he had been in a very bad mood, he could even have pulled out a gun and shot him.

Instead, Red Jelly frowned.

Then he opened his mouth and said a single word.

'Bingo?'

Chapter 25

When Red Jelly was a boy, he owned a dog.

A cute little puppy named Bingo.

Bingo was a small dog. Not too small, of course. But not too big either. In fact, he was just about the perfect size for a dog. He had black fur with a few white patches and a perky little tail, which wagged when he was happy and slumped between his legs when he was sad.

Red Jelly had loved Bingo more than anyone or anything else in the world.

Every day, he and Bingo had played in the yard. Every night, Bingo had slept on the end of his bed.

Bingo was the best friend that Red Jelly had ever had.

In fact, he was just about Red Jelly's only friend.

Of course, Red Jelly wasn't called Red Jelly then. He hadn't suffered his terrible accident. His body wasn't red. Nor was his face. His frame hadn't yet swelled up to an enormous size. He was just a miserable kid, living a miserable life with his miserable family. He was small and skinny and quite ordinary. No one thought he would ever amount to much. No one could have guessed that he would grow up to become the most famous criminal in Australia.

Now, Red Jelly looked at the little dog on the stage of the Sydney Opera House and found himself transported back in time to the days when he shared his life with

Bingo. He remembered how happy they had been together. He thought back to long afternoons when they had rolled in the dust, or chased rabbits in the paddocks. Then he remembered the way that Bingo would look and beg and bark when his belly was empty and his mouth was dry.

This little dog looked strangely similar to Bingo.

He wasn't Bingo. Of course he wasn't. Red Jelly was sure of that. He had buried Bingo himself many years ago. This dog was just another dog who happened to look a little like him.

But what was he doing here?

Red Jelly smiled.

He knew he shouldn't be smiling. He should be concentrating on his work. When you're a burglar or a bank robber or a kidnapper holding three thousand hostages, you shouldn't allow yourself to be distracted by cute puppies or pretty girls or anything else. You should just think about your job.

But Red Jelly couldn't help himself. He remembered Bingo. That cute little puppy. And how happy they had been together.

Red Jelly leaned down and looked at the dog. Then he unclipped his microphone so the audience couldn't hear what he was saying.

'I know what you want,' said Red Jelly. 'You're hungry, aren't you?'

Grk wagged his tail.

'I thought so,' said Red Jelly. He reached into his pocket, pulled out a hazelnut and threw it up in the air.

Grk watched the progress of the hazelnut very carefully. At precisely the correct moment, he sprang forward, opened his mouth, caught the nut and swallowed it in one quick gulp. Then he sat down, put his head on one side and begged again.

'You want another?' said Red Jelly.

Grk wagged his tail.

'Then you'd better have one.' Red Jelly tossed a second hazelnut into the air.

Grk caught it and ate it.

Around the vast auditorium, a few people laughed uncertainly. Some of them started to wonder if the whole thing had been a joke. Perhaps this wasn't really a robbery or a siege. Perhaps it was actually a piece of performance art. They weren't in danger at all. They were just getting an extra show, which had been included in the price of the ticket.

Red Jelly laughed too. He was enjoying himself. He threw another hazelnut to the dog, followed by a few more.

Grk jumped into the air again and again, grabbing each hazelnut and gulping it down.

Someone clapped. Then others joined in. And soon a vast wave of applause spread through the auditorium. Three thousand people cheered and whistled and stamped their feet, applauding the antics of a fat man and a little white dog.

Suddenly there was a loud BANG!

And the clapping stopped.

Chapter 26

Red Jelly pointed the pistol at the roof. He had fired once, but there was no need to fire again. The audience was quiet. Everyone was looking at him, waiting to hear what he said next.

Grk was looking at him too, hoping for another chocolate-coated hazelnut. He had eaten the whole packet, but he still had room in his stomach for more.

'Thank you,' said Red Jelly. He had clipped his microphone back on. Now his deep voice boomed from every loudspeaker in the auditorium. 'This is a very special evening, my friends. You've been raising money for some wonderful charities and you've had lots of fun. Now it's time to get serious.'

He stood there for a moment, looking at the enormous audience, the crowd of rich and successful people, the highest of Australia's high society. They lived in big houses protected by tall walls and strong gates. You wouldn't usually see them walking down the street or buying their food in a supermarket. They were too rich and too busy and too important to worry themselves with such stuff.

Well, today was different.

Today, Red Jelly didn't have to switch on the TV and listen to them talking about the economy or the crime rate or global warming. Today, they had to listen to him.

'As you must have guessed, this is a robbery,' said Red Jelly. 'My men are now going to hand out some bags. Please put your valuables inside. We'd like your jewellery, please, your purses and wallets too. Your phones, your pens and pencils, your tie clips and cuff links. Take them off and put them in the bag. Do you understand?'

He looked at the audience for a moment. No one spoke. No one even nodded or shook their heads. But they all understood what he had said.

'Here's a piece of advice,' said Red Jelly. 'Whatever you do, don't try to cheat me. I want *everything*, please. Your cash and your credit cards, your diamond chokers and your pearl earrings – I want them all. For your own safety, don't hide anything. We're going to search you later. If we discover that you've been hiding anything from us, you know what we'll do?'

Rather than answering, he lifted his pistol and pointed it into the audience.

'That's right,' he said. 'We'll blow your brains out.'

Red Jelly had twenty men positioned around the auditorium. They were dressed in black uniforms and armed with guns and grenades. Each of them looked like an efficient and highly-trained soldier.

Now they reached into their rucksacks and pulled out black bags. They walked down the aisles and handed the bags to the people sitting at the ends of the rows. Each person, they explained, should fill the bag with his or her valuables, then pass it on. The full bags would be collected at the opposite end of the row.

There were three thousand men and women in the audience. If they had worked together, they could have overcome Red Jelly and his men. Some of them would have been shot, of course. And there was always the risk of being blown up. But if they had charged forwards together, they could have beaten their common enemy.

But they didn't charge because they didn't want to get shot or blown up. Instead, some of them took the bags that had been given out. Others wept or closed their eyes. The rest of them sat in silence and waited to hear what Red Jelly was going to say next.

But Red Jelly didn't speak.

He just kneeled down and tickled Grk's ears.

Grk rolled over onto his belly and waggled his tail. Then he rolled back and begged.

'Sorry,' said Red Jelly. 'You've finished the lot.'

You're probably shocked that Grk was taking treats from an evil criminal.

Well, it is shocking.

But he was very hungry.

And he had another excuse too.

He didn't know that Red Jelly was evil.

Grk is only a dog, you see. And dogs don't know the difference between right and wrong. As far as Grk was concerned, his belly was empty. Nothing else mattered to him. He just wanted something to eat.

If Red Jelly had threatened his family or friends, of course he would have felt very differently. If Tim or Natascha or Max had been in the audience, he wouldn't have rolled on his belly or begged for a chocolate-coated hazelnut. If Red Jelly had shot at Tim's head or threatened to hurt Natascha or Max, then Grk would have been the first to bury his teeth in Red Jelly's ankles. He was ready and willing to give up his own life for those he loved. But he didn't know any of the people in the Opera House, just as he didn't know Red Jelly either. He didn't know which of them was good and which was bad and he didn't understand anyone was under threat. He just knew that he was hungry. And so he begged and simpered and rolled on the floor, wagging his tail and hoping to be given another treat.

Red Jelly tickled Grk's ears one last time, then stood up and stared at the audience.

He could see a wealthy couple sitting not far from the stage. A bald old man with a red nose and big ears was reluctantly picking through the contents of his jacket, looking at his plump leather wallet, his gold-plated pen and his platinum cuff links, knowing that he would never see them again.

Beside him, a grey-haired old woman in a velvet frock was unclipping a pearl choker from her skinny neck and slipping a pair of gold bands from her wrinkled wrists.

All around the auditorium, the same scenes were being repeated. Elegant women were unpicking their earrings and necklaces, their brooches and their bracelets. Sleek men were reaching into their pockets. The black bags were getting fuller and fuller.

Red Jelly smiled. He liked what he was seeing. Every minute, he was getting richer.

But now he had to escape.

He opened his mouth and spoke into his microphone. 'Hello, my friends. Could I have your attention for a moment, please?'

His voice boomed throughout the auditorium, amplified by speakers in every corner of the room.

'I'd like to invite four very important people to join me on the stage. The Mayor of Sydney, Mr Jimmy Hu. The Chief Executive of the Bank of Australia, Mrs Rebecca Ward. The Managing Director of the Corrigan Media Group, Mr Robert Corrigan. And, last but certainly not least, the Chairman of the Anglo-Australian Committee for International Business Cooperation, Sir Tristram Tinderbiscuit. Could all four of you come up here, please?'

Five minutes later, three men and a woman were standing on the stage, staring nervously at Red Jelly, wondering why he had called out their names.

Red Jelly stared back at his four hostages: the banker, the media mogul, the Mayor of Sydney and the diplomat. All of them were sleek, smart and very well dressed. They had expensive clothes and expensive shoes and expensive haircuts and expensive smiles. They were the type of people who were used to getting their own way.

Not tonight.

Unclipping his microphone, Red Jelly leaned forward and spoke in a low voice that could only be heard by his four hostages.

'Good evening,' he said. 'Do you know who I am?'

The three Australians nodded. They knew all about Red Jelly. In fact, they had recognised him already.

Sir Tristram Tinderbiscuit shook his head. 'Sorry, old chap. Not a clue. Must have missed the briefing.'

'Let me tell you about myself, Sir Tristram. My name is Red Jelly and I'm an ordinary bloke who wants to earn a few dollars so he can buy a beer or two and have some fun with his mates. That's what I'm doing tonight. And you're going to help me.'

'Help you?' Sir Tristram blinked. He wasn't quite sure that he had heard correctly. He'd only been in Australia for a few weeks and he still wasn't used to the local accent. 'How do you expect *me* to help *you*?'

'It's very simple, Sir Tristram. You're my ticket out of here.'

Chapter 27

Sirens filled the air. Police came from all directions. Cars screeched to a halt. Vans disgorged men and women with rifles and pistols and bulletproof jackets.

For years, the New South Wales Police Force had been training for an event like this. For years they had been imagining how to prevent a major terrorist incident. They had practised how to deal with a hijacked aeroplane at the airport or a ferry packed with hostages adrift in the bay. Once or twice, they had even rehearsed what they would do if someone put a bomb inside the Opera House.

Now their moment had arrived. Their opponent had finally announced himself. He had made his move. And they were ready for him. As soon as the order went out, the officers had grabbed their guns and their jackets and jumped into their vans.

Now they were here. The Opera House was surrounded. The roads were blocked. The air was guarded. The sea too.

No one could come in or go out.

Marksmen took up their positions and peered through their telescopic sights, searching for a target. Helicopters hovered overhead. Boats bobbed in the harbour with officers lining the sides, holding guns and binoculars, and waiting for instructions.

*

Chief Inspector Sam Somerville was in charge of the operation. He knew what he had to do. He had practised many times, preparing himself and his force for a situation like this. He ordered his men and women into position. He also sent an urgent recall to all off-duty officers, summoning them back to work – Australia needed them. Sydney needed them. And, most of all, three thousand people trapped inside the Opera House needed them.

A phone rang. A junior officer picked it up. He listened for a moment then looked at his boss. 'Chief Inspector? It's the call.'

'Thank you,' said Chief Inspector Somerville. 'I'll take it on this phone.'

Since the beginning of the siege, Chief Inspector Somerville had been waiting for 'the call'. Now he picked up the phone. He took a deep breath. Then he said: 'This is Chief Inspector Sam Somerville. Who am I speaking to?'

'Oh, come on, Sam,' said the voice on the other end of the line. 'Why don't you just say hello? We're old mates, aren't we?'

'No, we're not,' said Chief Inspector Somerville. 'If we're anything, we're old enemies.'

'I suppose you're right,' said Red Jelly. 'If you were really my mate, you wouldn't keep putting me in prison.'

'And if you were my mate, you wouldn't keep escaping.'

'It's the food,' said Red Jelly. 'I have to tell you, mate, the food in Australian prisons is just terrible. Make the food a bit better and maybe I won't have to keep escaping.'

'Thanks for that piece of advice,' said the Chief Inspector. 'Now, what are you doing in the Opera House? Why have you taken all these hostages? Why don't you just let them go?'

'I will,' said Red Jelly. 'As soon as you give me four choppers.'

'Four? Why do you need four?'

'I'll tell you in a minute, mate,' said Red Jelly. 'Now, let me tell you about these choppers. I want each of them to be loaded with enough fuel to fly six hundred kilometres. I want them to be delivered to the Opera House at eight o'clock in the morning. I want me and my team to be allowed to get aboard them. And then I want to fly away without any interference from the army, the police or anyone else. And, most importantly, I don't want you to put any trackers or bugs on these choppers. Because if you do, there'll be trouble. Did you get all that?'

'You're making a big mistake,' said Chief Inspector Somerville. 'Why don't you just let the hostages go and surrender yourself right now?'

Red Jelly just laughed. 'You think I want to go back to prison?'

'You're going back to prison whether you like it or not,' said Chief Inspector Somerville.

'That's what you think,' said Red Jelly. 'Now, listen to this. I'm going to give myself a little insurance policy, all right? I'm going to keep four of the hostages. When I leave in the helicopters, I'll take them with me. Just to make sure that you don't break your promises. When

I'm satisfied you haven't followed me, I'll let them go. You know what will happen to them if you do follow me?'

'You'd better not hurt them,' said the Chief Inspector.

'Then you'd better not follow me. Now, Sam, I want you to make me a promise. You'll get me these choppers, won't you?'

'I'll see what I can do.'

'And you won't mess me around, will you?'

'Of course not.'

'No trackers? No tricks? No funny games?'

'There'll be no trackers, no tricks and no funny games, I can promise you that.'

'Thanks, mate.'

'Stop calling me mate.'

'Sorry, mate. I'll call again in an hour or two, see how you're getting on. Goodnight, Sam.'

The line went dead.

Chief Inspector Somerville took another deep breath. Then he put down the phone and wondered what he was going to do.

Chapter 28

At the end of the day, Tim was escorted to the school gates by a teacher, who waited with him until he had been delivered into his mother's hands.

The headmaster wasn't taking any chances. He had instructed all his staff to keep a good eye on Tim. He didn't want one of his pupils to go missing. The school's reputation might never recover.

Mrs Malt was very relieved to see her son. She had half-expected to be greeted by a tearful teacher telling her that Tim had disappeared.

As they walked to the car, Mrs Malt said, 'How was school?'

'A complete waste of time,' said Tim.

'Oh,' said Mrs Malt. 'Why?'

'Because I had to sit in a stupid class and do stupid lessons with my stupid teachers when I should have been looking for Grk. Has anything happened? Has anyone found him yet?'

'I'm afraid not,' said Mrs Malt. 'I spoke to Mr Cuddle about an hour ago. They're still looking. They're very confident they'll find him soon.'

Tim just sighed. He didn't trust the Cuddles. They'd lost Grk in the first place. Why would they be able to find him?

Back home, Mrs Malt went upstairs to do some work,

leaving Tim alone. He fetched a glass of orange juice from the fridge, threw himself on the big, squashy sofa in the sitting room and searched for the remote control.

Usually, Grk would be sitting beside him. Being alone felt horrible. Doing nothing felt even worse. But he didn't know what else to do. How could he help Grk? What could he do?

Nothing. Not till later, anyway, when his parents were asleep. Then he would sneak out of the house and go to Cuddles Kennels and search for Grk himself. Till then, he just had to wait.

So he might as well watch TV.

He couldn't find the remote control. He pulled away the cushions and checked the back of the sofa. Then he looked *under* the sofa. Grk sometimes hid things there: slippers, bones, biscuits, stuff like that. And, indeed, that was exactly where Tim found the remote control, along with a tennis ball, two squares of chocolate and lots of fluff.

As he was sitting down again, he noticed a light flashing on the answerphone and immediately felt furious with himself. Why hadn't he listened to the message before? What if someone had found Grk?

He pressed PLAY.

There were two messages. The first one was from a man with an Australian accent.

'G'day. This is a message for Tim. It's Shane here. We met in Brazil. I'm in Sydney right now and... Well, this probably sounds really strange, but have you lost your dog? Because I think I've found him.'

106

The Australian man left his number and asked Tim to call him.

The second message was from Natascha. 'Hello, everyone. I wondered if there was any news. I wish I was there with you. Maybe I should come back to London. Anyway, I hope you're all OK. Let's speak soon. Bye.'

Tim saved both messages, then played the first one again. Then he played it once more. And then he went to find his mother.

'Mum,' he said. 'Mum!'

Mrs Malt was staring at her laptop, finishing some work. 'Yes, dear?'

'I know where Grk is.'

'You do? Where is he?'

'Sydney.'

'Did you say Sydenham?'

'No, I said Sydney.'

'Where's Sydney?'

'It's the capital of Australia.'

'Oh, no, it's not,' said Mrs Malt. 'Canberra is the capital of Australia. Sydney is simply the largest city. You should pay more attention in your geography lessons.'

'Whatever,' said Tim. 'The point is, Grk's there. There's a message on the answerphone. Someone's found him.'

'All alone, he travelled halfway around the world and he's now in Sydney, Australia?'

'Exactly.'

Mrs Malt sighed. 'Tim, have you finished your homework?'

'What do you mean?'

'I mean, have you done every piece of work that your teacher asked you to do?'

'I don't have time for homework,' said Tim. 'Even if I did, I wouldn't do it. I want to get Grk back. We have to call the police. We should ring the Australian High Commission. We have tell someone what's—'

'That's enough,' interrupted his mother. 'I'm sorry, Timothy, but I don't want to hear any more of your silly stories. In fact, I don't want to hear another squeak out of you till supper time. Go on, go upstairs and finish your homework.'

'Will you just come and listen to the message?'

'Which message?' said Mrs Malt.

'On the answerphone.'

'I will,' said Mrs Malt. 'But only when you've finished your homework.'

'Fine,' said Tim. 'Whatever.'

Leaving his mum with her laptop, Tim returned to the answerphone. He listened to the message twice more, copying down Shane's number and making sure that he'd written every numeral correctly. Then he picked up the phone and rang Australia.

It rang three times and then a bleary voice said, 'What time is it?'

'Five o'clock,' said Tim. 'Maybe six.'

'Five? Strewth! Who are you and why are you ringing me at five in the morning?'

'Oh,' said Tim. Of course, he thought. Australia is on the opposite side of the world. The middle of our afternoon is the middle of their night. 'I'm very sorry. I don't know the time in Sydney. It's tea time where I am.'

'Where are you, mate?'

'London.'

'London.' There was a moment's silence. Then Shane said, 'This isn't Tim, is it?'

'It is,' said Tim.

'Tim! Good to hear from you, mate! You got my message, then?'

'I did,' said Tim. 'Is Grk with you?'

'No, mate, he's not.'

'Where is he?'

'I wish I knew. Listen, mate, this is all very strange. You are the same Tim, right? The boy from Brazil.'

'I'm not from Brazil,' said Tim. 'I'm from England.'

'But you were in Brazil, right? We met there, didn't we?'

'That's right. You saved my life.'

'So I did, mate. So I did. You owe me one.'

'One what?' said Tim.

'One, er... I don't know. It's just a phrase.'

'A favour?' suggested Tim.

'I suppose so,' said Shane.

'I owe you another now. You've found Grk!'

'I haven't exactly found him,' said Shane. 'Well, I did find him. But now he seems to have lost himself again.'

'What do you mean? Where is he? What's happened?'

'Give me a chance and I'll tell you.'

Shane explained how he had met Grk in the middle of

the airport, just as he was about to check the engine on his chopper. He described the sudden arrival of the Dog Unit and the equally sudden disappearance of the little white dog.

'Sensible bloke, your dog,' said Shane. 'When he saw two guys with guns, he didn't want to stick around.'

Shane had searched the helicopter for Grk, wondering if he might have found a hiding place under a seat or even in the engine, but there was no sign of him. He was just wondering whether to search in the hangar or the other helicopters when his passengers arrived. He couldn't ask them to wait while he looked for a lost dog – billionaires and businesswomen don't like waiting for anyone. Shane ferried them to the business district and by the time he brought them back to the airport, the little white dog had long gone.

'I had a look around,' said Shane. 'But I couldn't see him anywhere. So I came home. Had a bite to eat, watched half a movie, fell asleep. Then some bloke woke me up.'

'I'm really sorry,' said Tim.

'No, no, I'm kidding. You did the right thing. You're worried about your dog. You want to find him again. Don't you?'

'Of course I do.'

'So, what are we going to do next? How are we going to find him?'

'Will you really help me?'

'That's what mates are for,' said Shane. 'If I was in trouble, you'd help me, wouldn't you?'

'I suppose so,' said Tim.

'Of course you would. You're in trouble, so I'll help you. Let me have a cup of coffee and a shower. I'm not used to waking up at five in the morning. When my brain is working a bit better, I'll call you back again. How does that sound?'

'That sounds great,' said Tim.

They said goodbye and ended the call.

Tim went to the kitchen and switched on the computer. If his mum questioned him, he would pretend that he was researching his geography homework and learning about Australia. He searched for information about Sydney, looking up the time difference, the weather and a map of the city. Then he wondered how to get there.

He could buy a flight.

But he didn't have enough pocket money, or a credit card.

His dad had a credit card. His mum too. He could get up in the middle of the night and steal one of them; he'd done it before and he wouldn't mind doing it again.

But he didn't have his passport. It was locked in his mother's desk and he didn't have the key. Even if he had a ticket, he wouldn't be allowed on a plane without a passport.

What else could he do?

He thought about the size of the Earth. He imagined the vast oceans and huge expanses of land that divided him from Grk. How could he possibly cross them and get to Sydney?

Even if he had a boat – and he didn't – sailing to Australia would take six months. By then, Grk would have vanished into the outback, never to be seen again.

A private jet could make the trip in a day or less, but he didn't know anyone with a private jet.

He couldn't possibly walk, drive, bike or hitchhike.

It was hopeless.

He knew where Grk was, but he couldn't do anything to help him.

Chapter 29

It was a long night for the hostages in the Sydney Opera House.

Filling the black bags took little more than an hour. After that, they had nothing to do.

Midnight passed. Then one o'clock. And two. And three.

Time ticked onwards towards dawn and still nothing happened. No one smashed down the doors. No one charged into the auditorium and rescued the hostages. There was no sign of the police. Red Jelly remained in control of the whole situation.

People slumped in their seats. They were hungry, thirsty, tired, frightened and beginning to despair. Some of them managed to sleep. Others simply stared blankly into space, so worried that they couldn't even close their eyes.

It was a long night for Rebecca Ward, Robert Corrigan, Jimmy Hu and Sir Tristram Tinderbiscuit, the four hostages who had been plucked out of the audience by Red Jelly. Now they sat in a corner of the stage, wondering why he had picked them.

What was he going to do with them?

Why had he said, 'You're my ticket out of here'?

What could that possibly mean?

The four of them were experienced and self-confident. They had been involved in big business deals and international incidents. But they had never had to face a situation like this.

They talked in low voices, discussing their options and trying to plan for every eventuality.

It was a long night for the police who were surrounding the Opera House.

They had arrived in cars, vans and helicopters, rushing into position and keeping the entire place under surveillance.

But then nothing happened.

Marksmen put down their rifles and flexed their fingers. Commanders pored over maps and discussed tactics. Officers drank cups of coffee and rubbed their eyes, trying to stay awake and alert.

The night wore on. The police stayed in position. But still nothing happened.

It wasn't a long night for Grk.

He was curled up on a corner of the stage. His eyes were closed, his belly was full of chocolate-coated hazelnuts and he was fast asleep. He could hardly have been happier.

Every now and then, he opened his eyes and looked around. He peered at the people in the auditorium, who were sleeping or whispering or praying quietly to themselves. He glanced at Sir Tristram Tinderbiscuit and the other three hostages squatting nearby, talking together in low voices. Then he closed his eyes and went back to sleep.

Chapter 30

Tim was thinking through his options, trying to come up with a plan, when the phone rang. He grabbed it. 'Hello?'

'Hi, Tim,' said Shane. 'How are you?'

'Not very good,' said Tim.

'Well, you might feel better when you hear my news.'

'Have you found Grk?'

'Not exactly.'

'What do you mean, "not exactly"? Have you found him or haven't you?'

'I haven't exactly found him, but I know where he is.'

'Where?'

'Turn on your TV and you'll find out.'

'The TV? Why?'

'Stop asking so many questions,' said Shane. 'Just find yourself a TV and turn it on.'

Tim grabbed the remote and switched on the TV. A black-and-white movie filled the screen. A cowboy was galloping through a narrow valley on a white horse. An arrow thumped into his shoulder. Tim said, 'What channel?'

'The one with Grk on,' said Shane.

Tim switched channels, wondering what he was supposed to be looking for. Anyway, why would Grk be on TV? And wouldn't the TV in Australia be showing different stuff from the TV in London? Shane sounded very sure of himself, so Tim didn't argue with him. He just kept clicking the remote control. He went past a gardening show and an auction show and the *Teletubbies*, but there was no sign of Grk. He went onwards, flicking past an old episode of *Friends* and a movie and another movie and a shopping channel selling garden furniture and a football match and more movies and more shopping channels and then he reached Sky News.

A newsreader was talking directly to the camera. Behind him, there was a picture of the Sydney Opera House. The newsreader was in mid-sentence:

'... inside the Opera House, but no one knows what he wants. For now, three thousand hostages simply have to wait and pray.'

Tim leaned forwards and stared at the TV.

At that moment, the picture changed. Now a different newsreader was smiling at the camera. Behind him, the screen was showing a picture of the Houses of Parliament. The newsreader said: 'We'll keep you updated on the developing situation in Australia throughout the day. Now, here in London, Parliament has been debating a controversial plan to introduce wild buffaloes into the Scottish Highlands.'

Tim pressed the button on the remote control, switching to another channel, then another, searching for more news. He finally found BBC News 24, which was showing some shaky footage filmed on a mobile phone. A newsreader's voice explained that this footage had

116

been filmed a few hours ago inside the Sydney Opera House.

A huge, red-faced man stood at the front of the stage, holding a pistol in his right hand. He was talking to the audience, lecturing them, threatening them, warning them about what would happen if they tried to fight or escape.

Suddenly, a small white dog wandered onto the stage. The red-faced man turned to look at him. He said a few words. The dog barked and wagged his tail. Then the fat man reached into his pocket. And threw something across the stage.

The little dog caught it in his mouth.

The picture changed. A newsreader was standing outside the Opera House, talking directly to the camera. Behind him the dark sky was lit up by the blue and red flashes of police lights, and Tim could see police officers milling around in the background. Some were armed with rifles. Others were wearing helmets and carrying riot shields.

The newsreader explained what was happening. An audacious criminal gang had taken three thousand people hostage inside the Sydney Opera House. The police had already established the identity of the gang's leader.

'His name is Red Jelly,' said the newsreader. The screen showed a picture of an enormously fat man with bright-red skin. 'He's one of most famous criminals in Australia, known to be responsible for at least eighty-seven separate robberies, and suspected of hundreds more. With him, he has a gang of at least twenty armed men. And a dog.'

The picture changed once more. Now the screen showed a photograph taken by one of the hostages inside the Opera House. There was Red Jelly. And there, standing beside him like a loyal pet with its master, was a small white dog.

Tim picked up the phone. 'Shane?'

'You've seen him?'

'It's amazing,' said Tim. 'How did Grk get in there?'

'No one knows, mate. But you'd better call the police. They'll want to know who he is.'

Chapter 31

Tim raced upstairs to find his mother.

'Mum,' he called. 'Mum!'

'Yes, dear?' Mrs Malt was still staring at her laptop, adjusting some figures in a spreadsheet.

'I know where Grk is.'

'Really?' said Mrs Malt, keying figures into the spreadsheet and hardly listening to her son. 'Where is he? Still in Sydenham?'

'He was never in Sydenham,' said Tim. 'He was in Sydney.'

'Oh, yes. And where is he now? The moon?'

'On TV. Will you come and watch?'

'Watch what?' said Mrs Malt.

'I just told you. Grk's on TV.'

'Oh, Tim. Stop fooling around. Have you finished your homework?'

'Please, Mum. Come and watch. It will only take two seconds.'

Mrs Malt sighed and shook her head. 'You don't seem to understand, Tim, how difficult it is to be a working mother. I'm trying to juggle seven different jobs at once. You want one thing. My boss wants another. Then there's Max and Natascha. And your father too. I wish I did have two seconds to spare, because I might be able to think of myself for a moment. As it is, every single second of my day seems to be taken up by someone else.'

'Mum. Please. You've got to see this.'

The tone of Tim's voice made Mrs Malt realise that he was serious. She paused for a moment, wondering what to do, then nodded. 'I'll come and have a look,' she said. 'But I hope you're not messing around, Tim. Because I'm really not in the mood for jokes.'

'Don't worry,' said Tim. 'Nor am I.'

Chapter 32

'It's the latest model, sir,' said Special Agent Anthony Pecorino. In his right hand, he was holding a small black disc, not much bigger than a coin and not much thicker either. 'It has a battery inside which will last about a month. It sends out a signal to a satellite in orbit above the planet. The signal bounces back to us, telling us its exact location.'

'That tiny thing,' said Chief Inspector Somerville, pointing at the disc. 'It can do all that?'

'And more,' said Special Agent Pecorino. 'It provides a wealth of information. But, most important, wherever it goes, we can follow it. You just have to let me hide it inside the chopper and these guys will never be able to escape from us.'

Chief Inspector Somerville shook his head. 'I can't let you do that.'

'Why not, sir?'

'I don't want to endanger the lives of the hostages.'

Special Agent Pecorino smiled and shook his head. He was used to people who didn't understand the wonderful possibilities of his trackers. 'Don't worry, sir. You won't be endangering anyone at all. Look at the size of this thing! When I've hidden this inside the chopper, Red Jelly will never find it. Not in a million years.'

'But what if he did?'

'He won't, sir. I can guarantee it. I've hidden these little lovelies everywhere and anywhere, and they've never been found. I've put them in cars and bikes. I've put them in suitcases and handbags. Once, I even put one in a shoe, a lady's shoe, and she never suspected a thing. I've followed suspects from one end of Australia to the other. And, I can promise you, sir, no one has ever found their tracker. No one even realised they were being followed. Look at this beauty, sir.' Special Agent Pecorino held out the tracker in the palm of his hand. 'It's so small, it's practically invisible.'

The door swung open, interrupting the conversation. A policewoman stepped into the room. 'Excuse me, sir. Can I have a word?'

'Can't you see we're busy?' said Chief Inspector Somerville, waving her away. 'Come back later.'

'It's about Red Jelly.'

The chief inspector whirled round, suddenly alert. 'What's happened?'

'We've had a message from a woman in London,' said the policewoman in a low voice. 'She says he's got her dog.'

'Who has?'

'Red Jelly, sir.'

'I thought you said she lives in London.'

'She does, sir. The dog seems to have escaped.'

'She's lost her dog in London and she thinks it's now in Sydney?'

'Yes, sir.'

'She's obviously crazy.'

'I think you should talk to her, sir.'

'I don't have time to talk to crazy people.'

'I know, sir. But I don't think she's crazy. I think she's telling the truth.'

The chief inspector sighed. 'Very well. Get her on the line. But you'd better not be wasting my time.'

'Thank you, sir. I'll put you through right now.' The policewoman picked up the phone on the desk and dialled a London number.

Special Agent Pecorino held up the small black disc. 'What about the tracker, sir?'

'What about it?'

'Well, sir, what do you want me to do? Shall I put it in the chopper?'

'Give me a minute to take this call,' said Chief Inspector Somerville. 'Then we'll decide what to do.'

Chief Inspector Sam Somerville had spent his entire career in the Australian police force. During that time, he had met a lot of crazy people.

Some of them were criminals. Others wanted to be criminals. They came into police stations all across the country and confessed to crimes that they hadn't committed. 'I've just murdered my sister,' they would say. An hour later, their sister would collect them from the station and take them home.

Over the years, Chief Inspector Sam Somerville had learned to recognise the crazy ones. He could hear the craziness in their voices and see the craziness in their eyes.

As soon as he spoke to Mrs Malt, he knew that she wasn't crazy.

She was saying some crazy things, yes, but she wasn't crazy.

He talked to her for five minutes, writing a few notes on a sheet of paper. Then he asked her to stay by the phone for the next hour.

'I'm not sure if I can do that,' said Mrs Malt. 'You see, I'm very busy. I have a lot of things to do. I've got to cook supper and help my son with his homework and finish my own work and—'

'Excuse me for interrupting,' interrupted Chief Inspector Somerville. 'I don't want to sound disrespectful in any way, but I have to say one thing, Mrs Malt. The current situation is a lot more important than your son's schoolwork or, to be honest, your own work either. Three thousand people are being held hostage inside Sydney Opera House. You might be able to help them. I don't know if you can, but just in case, couldn't you stay by the phone for the next hour?'

Mrs Malt agreed that she could.

The Chief Inspector rang three of his best officers and ordered them to investigate the dog story. He told them that he wanted results within fifteen minutes. Then he called in a technician and asked to see several snippets from the Opera House news footage.

'Excuse me, sir?' Special Agent Pecorino held up the tracker. 'Have you made a decision, sir?'

'Not now,' said the Chief Inspector.

'But, sir, if I'm going to put it in the chopper, I need to—'

'I said, not now.' The Chief Inspector waved him away. 'We'll talk about the tracker later. Right now, I need to think. Could you come back in a couple of hours?'

'Yes, sir.' Special Agent Pecorino sighed. No one seemed to appreciate all his hard work. His trackers were the best in the world. They were reliable, accurate and practically invisible. But, once again, he had been dismissed without a second thought. He dropped the small black disc into his jacket pocket and sloped out of the room.

As soon as Pecorino had gone, the Chief Inspector sat down at his computer. The technician had sent over the footage that he wanted. For the next few minutes, the Chief Inspector watched Red Jelly tossing chocolate-coated hazelnuts to a little white dog, then kneeling on the stage and tickling the dog's belly.

A little white dog...

Over the years, Chief Inspector Somerville had read Red Jelly's file many times. He almost knew it off by heart. So he knew all about the little dog.

Red Jelly had been a very unhappy child. His father had beaten him almost every day. His mother had neglected him. He had been unloved and perhaps even unwanted.

He was kicked out of one school, then another. Wherever he went, he learned to look after himself with his fists, settling arguments with violence rather than words. He quickly earned a reputation as a troublemaker. When schools started refusing to take him, he spent his time hanging out on the streets instead. That was where he learned how to be a criminal.

Throughout his lonely and miserable childhood, Red Jelly only ever had one friend.

A small dog named Bingo.

There wasn't a picture of Bingo in the file, but there was a description of him.

The Chief Inspector stared at the dog on the screen.

That dog wasn't Bingo. He couldn't be. It was impossible. Dogs don't live very long. Bingo must be dead by now.

But, according to the description in the file, Bingo was pretty much a perfect match for the dog on the screen. Somehow, somewhere, Red Jelly had managed to find himself a second Bingo.

Precisely fifteen minutes after he had issued his orders, Chief Inspector Sam Somerville received phone calls from the three officers who had been researching the story of the dog. Each of them explained what he had discovered.

The first officer had spoken to Trevor Cuddle and confirmed that Grk had escaped from Cuddles Kennels on Sunday morning. He had also quizzed security guards in the airport, who agreed that a dog might possibly have managed to sneak into the luggage compartment of a plane.

The second officer told him that a stray dog had caused chaos at Kingsford Smith Airport on Monday afternoon. No one knew the identity of the dog, but it appeared to have escaped from a British Airways flight, which had recently arrived from London.

The third officer had spoken to a pilot who was currently working for Botany Bay Air Taxis. His name was Shane and he knew all about Grk.

When Chief Inspector Somerville had spoken to his three officers, he rang London again. He talked to Mrs Malt, describing what he had discovered and asking her to come to Sydney.

'How can I come to Sydney?' cried Mrs Malt. 'It's on the other side of the world!'

'I know it's a long way,' said Chief Inspector Somerville. 'I'm sure you're very busy and you have some very important things to do today. But we have an extraordinary situation here in Sydney. A very dangerous man is on the loose. Many innocent people are in danger. We have to save them. Now, there is a possibility that you might be able to help us. It's a slim possibility, I know. But, to me, that doesn't matter. What I think is this: we must do whatever it takes to stop this criminal and save the lives of his hostages. Don't you agree?'

Chapter 33

Chief Inspector Somerville had said he would get seats for Tim and his mother organised on the next available flight. So while Mrs Malt was hurriedly packing bags for them, Tim grabbed a spare lead and collar for Grk.

He wondered whether to take some dog biscuits or a tin of dog food, but decided not to bother. He'd be able to buy some in Australia. He was sure Australian dogs would eat pretty much the same food and biscuits as dogs anywhere else in the world.

His mum still hadn't finished packing, so he went downstairs, picked up the phone and called Stanislavia.

After three rings, a female voice answered in Stanislavian.

Tim didn't have a clue what the voice was saying. He couldn't speak more than a few words in Stanislavian and he wasn't even sure that he pronounced them correctly. So he spoke in English, saying, 'Hello, this is Tim. Can I speak to Max or Natascha, please?'

'Hello, Tim. This is Irena, the cousin of Max and Natascha. How are you?'

'Very well, thanks,' said Tim. 'How are you?'

'I am excellent, thank you.'

Tim knew Irena didn't speak very good English, so he talked slowly and carefully, hoping she would understand him. 'Irena, please will you give a message to Max and Natascha?'

'Yes, of course. What is your message?'

'I am going to Australia and I will not come back till I have found Grk. Do you understand?'

'I understand completely,' said Irena. 'You go to Australia and you come back with Grk. But I must ask one question. Why Grk is in Australia?'

'It's a long story,' said Tim.

Mr Malt had come home from work as soon as he heard what had happened. He and Mrs Malt discussed whether they should both go to Australia, but they decided that one of them should stay at home. When all the bags were packed, Mr Malt drove his wife and his son to Heathrow Airport.

He dropped them at Departures. He kissed Mrs Malt and hugged Tim and told them both to look after themselves. Then he stood by the car, watching them walk across the road and through the sliding doors, waiting till he could no longer see them.

Inside the airport, Mrs Malt led Tim to the Cathay Pacific Information Desk and said, 'Hello, my name is Melanie Malt. I was told that someone would be waiting for me here.'

A tall man in a dark suit stepped forwards. He had a little grey moustache, a confident smile and an Australian accent. 'Hello, Mrs Malt. And you must be Tim? Pleased to meet you both. My name is Charlie Cecconi. I work at the Australian High Commission here in London. Now, if you don't mind, we'd better hurry along. The plane is twenty-five minutes late already. They've been holding it for you. This way, please.'

Charlie Cecconi whisked Tim and Mrs Malt through passport control and three different security checks, then led them through endless long white corridors until they arrived at the back entrance of a boarding gate. He ushered them onto the plane, wished them luck and said goodbye.

An air steward welcomed Tim and his mother aboard and took them to their seats in the first-class cabin. The doors were closed and the aircraft was prepared for take-off. Ten minutes later, the plane taxied along the runway and lifted into the air.

They were on their way to Singapore. There, the plane would refuel, before continuing on to Australia. This time tomorrow, they would be in Sydney.

Chapter 34

It was early in the morning of a perfect day. Sydney looked beautiful. The sun was shining, the sky was clear and the Australian police were absolutely furious.

They were hungry too, and very tired. But mostly they were furious.

They had stayed in position overnight, hunched behind barricades, clutching their rifles and their bullet-proof shields, watching the Opera House and waiting for the Red Jelly Gang to make their next move.

Not long after dawn, the city had come to life around them. They saw the first commuters crossing the harbour on ferries. The windows of nearby office blocks crowded with faces, peering down at the Opera House, watching the scene of the siege.

Now, finally, things were happening.

Helicopters were landing. Hostages were emerging. Criminals too.

But the police had been given strict orders to keep away. A message had come directly from Chief Inspector Somerville. Don't shoot, he'd said. Don't even move from your positions. Just stay still and watch and wait for further orders.

Red Jelly's men emerged from the Opera House, bringing bag after bag of loot and loading them into the four helicopters.

Along with the bags, the Red Jelly Gang led four hostages out of the Opera House, three men and a woman. One of the hostages clambered into each of the helicopters and took a seat opposite an armed member of the gang.

The police watched. And waited. And did nothing.

Marksmen were poised, their eyes pressed to telescopic sights, their fingers curled around triggers. With a few well-placed bullets, they could have picked off every criminal leaving the Opera House.

A thousand police could have rushed forward and arrested every member of the Red Jelly Gang.

But they followed orders and did nothing.

The doors slid shut. The rotors whirred. The helicopters lifted into the air and flew across the harbour.

Grk was confused.

He had been promised breakfast. He thought he had, anyway. The fat man had said, 'Come on, Bingo. Come here! Follow me, mate!'

Grk followed him. Of course he did. Where else was he going to find some more of those delicious chocolate-coated hazelnuts? It was the morning now and he hadn't eaten anything since the night before. He would happily follow anyone who could fill his stomach.

Together, Grk and the fat man trotted down a narrow corridor and through a doorway and across a yard and into a small machine, which smelled of oil.

Grk looked around, but he couldn't see any sign of breakfast.

Inside the small machine, the fat man sat down and strapped a seatbelt around his enormous belly. Grk squatted at his feet, wondering when they were going to serve the hot buttered toast.

There was a terrible noise. Which got louder and louder. And then the whole world suddenly shot into the air. Grk scrambled for safety. He lurched under the seat and jammed himself there, his feet pinned to the floor, waiting for the world to stop moving.

Sitting in the seat directly above him, Red Jelly leaned back and folded his burly arms across his enormous chest.

Red Jelly had been awake all night, but he wasn't tired. He didn't even want to go to sleep yet. He was too excited.

Everything was working perfectly. Just as he had planned.

With a wide smile on his face, he looked out of the window, staring down at the city of Sydney, spread out underneath him.

He thought about the four helicopters filled with men and hostages, flying in formation towards the Blue Mountains. He thought about the black bags packed with money and jewels. He thought about the news broadcasts all around the world, showing an image of his face and describing the fabulous crime that he had just committed.

His smile grew even wider.

Down on the ground, Chief Inspector Somerville lifted his binoculars to his eyes and watched the four helicopters cruise through the sky.

He didn't know where they were going. Even worse, he didn't have any way to find out.

He had kept his promise. His men hadn't placed any bugs or trackers on board any of the helicopters. He didn't want to take any risks with the lives of four very important hostages.

He hoped he hadn't made a terrible mistake.

The Blue Mountains is a vast area of steep-sided hills and deep, narrow valleys to the west of Sydney. That was where the helicopters disappeared.

They didn't really disappear, of course. They just disappeared from the screens of anyone who was trying to track them.

One moment, radar operators could see four blips on their screens. The next moment, the four blips had vanished.

Dodging radar isn't complicated. You just have to fly very close to the ground. As the four choppers wove through the valleys of the Blue Mountains, that was exactly what they did.

When they flew into the outback, the four pilots stayed at the same height. They skimmed along, only a metre or two above the ground, dodging trees, slaloming round bushes, hugging the earth.

Up ahead, there was a vast emptiness.

*

Australia is the sixth largest country on the planet.

(Just in case you're wondering, the five bigger countries are Russia, Canada, China, the USA and Brazil, in that order.)

In this enormous country there aren't actually very many people – only twenty million of them, in fact. That's not much more than the population of Los Angeles or Tokyo.

Almost all these twenty million Australians live in a handful of big cities: Sydney, Brisbane, Melbourne, Adelaide, Darwin and Perth.

If you look at a map, you'll notice that all six of those cities are on the coast. Most Australians live within spitting distance of the sea.

If you go inland, you'll find a few roads, a few lizards, a lot of sheep. And not much else.

It's a very good place to hide.

Chapter 35

That night, representatives of the Bank of Australia met representatives of the Mayor's office, the Corrigan Media Group and the Anglo-Australian Committee for International Business Cooperation. They discussed the best way to help Rebecca Ward, Jimmy Hu, Robert Corrigan and Sir Tristram Tinderbiscuit. After a long conversation, they decided to offer a reward to be given in exchange for any information leading to the capture of Red Jelly. Between them, they donated a million Australian dollars.

Posters were printed. Emails were sent out. News bulletins spread the word. All over Australia – and all around the world – people saw the same message:

REWARD
ONE MILLION DOLLARS
FOR ANY INFORMATION LEADING TO
THE CAPTURE OF THE NOTORIOUS CRIMINAL
SIDNEY ARTHUR O'SULLIVAN
ALSO KNOWN AS
RED JELLY

The poster featured two photographs of Red Jelly.

In the first, he was staring directly into the camera, his red face splintered by a broad smile. He looked proud, confident and very happy. Come and get me, he seemed to be saying. Catch me if you can.

In the second, taken only a day ago, he was standing on the stage of the Sydney Opera House. The picture showed his enormous body, his unmistakable bulk, his bulging belly and his thick thighs straining to break through his black clothes. Standing at his feet, looking up at his face, there was a small white dog.

At first, the citizens of Sydney were the only people looking for Red Jelly and his little white dog. They wanted to find the fat man and the dog who had besieged their opera house.

But news spread fast. Messages flashed across the country and around the world. A million dollars is a lot of money. Minute by minute, hour by hour, more and more people joined the search.

Soon, the inhabitants of Adelaide and Canberra were hunting for Red Jelly and his little white dog. Then the citizens of Perth and Brisbane joined in. And so did everyone else in Australia. Wherever they lived, they searched their neighbourhood for an enormous red-faced man and a little white dog, hoping to catch a crook and earn a reward of one million dollars.

But where was the Red Jelly Gang? Where had they flown in those four helicopters?

North, south, east, west?

Up to Darwin? Down to Melbourne?

Did they try to reach the coast and catch a boat and head for another country where they wouldn't be so famous?

Did they have a plane stored somewhere, waiting to take them to the other side of the world?

Or did they go deeper and deeper into the heart of the vast scrubby outback, the empty heart of Australia, where you could hide for years, never meeting another human being?

At twenty-past three on Tuesday afternoon, a man named William Priest rang the police and said, 'I've found him.'

'Found who?' asked the operator.

'That crook's dog! I've found him! Do I get a million dollars now?'

'You will, sir. If he's the right dog and leads us to Red Jelly. Where exactly did you see him?'

'He's tied up outside the post office.'

'Which post office?'

'In Katoomba, of course.'

'You're in Katoomba now, are you?'

'Where else would I be? I'm Katoomba through and through. Born here, bred here, probably die here too. Anyway, what are you going to do about this dog? You're going to look him up, aren't you?'

'We'll send someone to check it.'

'You'd better be quick, sweetheart. What if Red Jelly

comes back? I don't want to tackle him myself. I'm not so fit as I used to be.'

'Have you actually seen Red Jelly in Katoomba?'

'No, no, but he must be here, right? If his dog is.'

A police unit was despatched immediately. Sirens wailing, the car roared through the streets of Katoomba and screeched to a halt outside the post office. Two policemen leaped out, guns drawn, and found an old lady, named Marjorie Clark, untying her dog Bonzer. She had left him outside the post office while she went to post a parcel to her sister in Hobart. The police checked Bonzer against a photograph of Grk and could see immediately that the two dogs were quite different. Bonzer was twice the size of Grk and mostly brown.

The police released Marjorie Clark and Bonzer, then had some stern words with William Priest on the subject of wasting police time.

Over the following few hours, more Grk-alikes were reported all around Australia. Six were sighted in Sydney. Another four were found in Melbourne. Yet more were spotted in Cannonvale, Mooloolaba, Port Augusta, Porongurup, Moreton Bay and the Yarrangobilly Caves. Someone even called the police from Kuala Lumpur, four thousand miles away from Sydney, claiming to have seen Grk riding in a taxi.

The police couldn't afford to ignore any of these reports; they didn't want to risk missing Red Jelly. Officers were despatched to every location, ready to do battle with twenty heavily armed criminals, their red-faced boss and his pet dog.

Some of the animals did actually look quite like Grk. Others bore no resemblance to him. But not one of them was Grk himself.

Chapter 36

A little after ten o'clock on Wednesday morning, several hundred newly arrived passengers at Kingsford Smith Airport were waiting in a very long line, queuing to show their documents at passport control.

An official in a dark suit walked along the line, looking at the faces of every passenger. He stopped beside two people near the very back of the queue, a woman and a boy.

'Mrs Melanie Malt?' he said. 'And Tim?'

'That's us,' said Mrs Malt.

'Welcome to Australia. Will you come with me, please?'

'Why?' said Mrs Malt. 'Who are you?'

'I work for the police. You're our guest in Australia, so we're going to take you straight to the front of the queue.'

Tim had a question. 'Have you got Grk?'

'Not yet, no. The Red Jelly Gang made a getaway in four helicopters, and they took Grk with them.'

'Where have they gone?'

'I can't give you that information right now,' said the official. 'When you see Chief Inspector Somerville this afternoon, he'll be able to tell you everything about the investigation.'

'This afternoon?' said Tim. 'Why do we have to wait till this afternoon?'

'The Chief Inspector has a very busy schedule. Now, will you follow me please? Let's get you into the country.'

The official led Tim and Mrs Malt to the front of the queue, taking them past the curious stares and resentful glares of the other passengers, who wondered, once again, what was so special about those two. Back in London, they had arrived late for the flight, which was delayed especially for them. They sat in first class. And now they had been met by an official in a dark suit and taken to the front of the queue at passport control. Who were they? A teenage pop star and his mum? Minor members of the royal family? Or just billionaires who could get whatever they wanted with a snap of their fingers?

I'm no one special, Tim wanted to say. And I'm sorry about the queue jumping. I'd be happy to wait like everyone else.

But he kept quiet and, following his mum's example, showed his passport to an officer in a blue uniform. The officer glanced at the passport and said, 'Welcome to Australia, Mr Malt.'

'Thanks very much,' said Tim, suddenly feeling rather grown-up. He didn't often get called 'Mr Malt.'

'This way, please,' said the official in the dark suit. He led Tim and Mrs Malt down a long white corridor to the luggage carousels. 'Now, I know you've had a very long flight, but I hope you're ready for a quick chat with the press. I don't know how they've done it, but they've somehow found out about your arrival.'

Tim was impatient to start searching for Grk, but he could see that there was no point arguing. He stood beside his mother, staring at the luggage carousel, waiting for their bags to emerge.

When the official had hauled each of their suitcases from the carousel and placed them on a trolley, he led them to the exit. They walked though a passage marked NOTHING TO DECLARE and emerged in the arrivals lounge. There they were greeted by thirty cameras and a barrage of shouting journalists.

'Mrs Malt! Mrs Malt! Over here!'

'Tim! Tim! Smile please!'

'Can you answer a question for the readers of the *Morning Herald*? Where did you get Grk?'

'What's his favourite food?'

'When did you first realise your dog had criminal tendencies?'

'Does he steal stuff at home?'

'Are you going to punish him?'

'How do you say his name?'

Mrs Malt was bewildered by the attention, but she quite enjoyed it too. She'd never been bombarded by questions like this before. She turned from journalist to journalist, answering their questions with what she hoped was a polite smile and a neat turn of phrase.

Tim didn't smile. Nor did he answer any of the stupid questions that he was asked. In fact, he wished he was somewhere else. He didn't want to be interviewed or photographed or featured on news bulletins. He just wanted to find Grk.

When the journalists and photographers had got what they wanted, the official led Tim and Mrs Malt to a large black car. They drove from the airport to the centre of Sydney, where the police had arranged for them to stay in adjoining rooms at one of the very smartest hotels in the city.

A car would pick them up at half-past two and drive them to their appointment with Chief Inspector Somerville. He would tell them everything about the current state of the police investigation. His officers would also want to ask all sorts of questions about Grk's character, habits and appearance. They wanted to know if Grk might be able to help them in any way in their search for Red Jelly and his four hostages.

Until then, Tim and Mrs Malt were free to spend their time however they wished. They could have a swim in the hotel's pool, order any number of delicacies from room service, wander round the city or just sleep.

Mrs Malt was exhausted and jet lagged from the long flight and she wanted to be alert for their meeting that afternoon with Chief Inspector Somerville, so she decided to have a snooze. She went to her room, climbed into bed and immediately fell into a deep sleep.

Tim was tired too, but he hadn't travelled halfway round the world to curl up under a sheet. Now he was here in Sydney, he wanted to find Grk.

He didn't know where to look. But he knew someone who might.

There was a phone beside the bed.

He pulled a scrap of paper from his pocket and dialled the number written on the paper.

'Hello?' said a voice.

'Is that Shane?'

'Hello, mate! Where are you?'

'In Sydney,' said Tim.

'Welcome to Aus, mate! How do you like it here?'

'I don't know,' said Tim. 'I haven't seen anything except the airport and the hotel, and they just look like airports and hotels.'

'You've got to get out more, mate. See some of Sydney. You've come to the most beautiful city on the planet! You can't just sit in your hotel room.'

'Actually,' said Tim, 'I don't want to see more of the city. I just want to find Grk.'

'Then you'd better come with me.'

'Do you know where he is?'

'Not yet, mate, but I'm going to find him.'

'How?'

'With the tracker, mate.'

'Which tracker?'

'The one in Red Jelly's helicopter.'

'Are you serious? There's a tracker in Red Jelly's helicopter?'

'That's right, mate.'

'But I talked to a policeman. He said it was too dangerous to try and track the helicopter. He said the Chief Inspector had decided not to even try.'

'That's what Chief Inspector Somerville might have decided,' said Shane. 'But someone else had a different idea.'

'Who?'

'This guy I know. We drink in the same pub. His

145

name's Tony Pecorino. He's a good bloke, for a cop, if you know what I'm saying. Anyway, he called me up. He said he needs my help. He's put a tracker on that chopper and he needs someone to follow it. A pilot. So he thought of me.'

'I don't understand,' said Tim. 'If he's a policeman, why did he put a tracker on the helicopter? I thought the police had decided not to.'

'He designed this tracker himself,' said Shane. 'He wants to prove it works. He wants to show the whole world that he can track down the Red Jelly Gang.'

'Won't he get in trouble?'

'Maybe he will, mate, but that's his problem. Unless you're worried about the cops?'

'I just want to find Grk,' said Tim.

'Me too, mate. That's why I'm going to grab a plane and follow the signal from Tony's tracker. Do you want to come with me?'

'Of course I do,' said Tim. For the first time in hours – no, the first time in days – he felt happy. He was finally, properly, on Grk's trail. 'When are you leaving?'

'As soon as you get here.'

'Where are you?'

'Do you know the airport?'

'I've just been there.'

'You'd better come back again. Take a cab. Ask them to drop you at Botany Bay Air Taxis. They'll know where it is. You'll find me here. But hurry, mate, we don't want to waste too much time.'

'I'll leave now,' said Tim. Then he thought of

something. 'There's just one problem,' he said. 'I don't have any Australian money.'

'No worries. I'll pay the driver when you get here.'

Tim said goodbye to Shane and put the phone down. He looked around the room, wondering if he needed to take anything with him. A change of clothes? A bottle of water? His passport? No, there was only one thing that he needed. A spare lead and a spare collar for Grk. He'd stuffed them in his bag before they left home. Now he grabbed them, put them in his pocket and headed for the door. Then he remembered his mum. Should he tell her what he was doing? Of course not. She'd never let him leave the hotel and go to find Shane. Should he leave her a note? No, that could wait. If she woke up, she'd just think he'd gone for a walk round the hotel. He could text her later and tell her what he was really doing. He tiptoed out of the room, closed the door behind him and hurried along the corridor.

Downstairs, Tim walked out of the air-conditioned hotel and into the heat of the day. A hotel porter nodded to him. 'Taxi, sir?'

'Yes, please,' said Tim.

The porter gestured to a waiting taxi. It purred forwards and drew to a halt beside them. The porter opened the back door for Tim. 'Have a good day, sir.'

'Thanks,' said Tim. He clambered into the cab and waited for the porter to close the door. He didn't want to leave any clues for anyone who tried to discover where he had gone. Then he said, 'The airport, please.'

Chapter 37

Tim and Shane hurried across the tarmac to a small twin-propeller aircraft with BBAT printed in large green letters on its side. Botany Bay Air Taxis owned several small planes as well as helicopters. A mechanic was tinkering with the engine. Shane nodded to him. 'Hello, mate. Is she ready to go?'

'Just about,' said the mechanic.

'Fuel full?'

'To the brim.'

'Excellent.' Shane opened the door and helped Tim aboard.

The mechanic consulted a sheet of paper. 'What are you doing, Shane? You're not on the schedule.'

'There's been a change of plan,' said Shane. 'I've got to give this kid a lift home. Talk to Tilly in the office, she'll tell you all about it.'

'No worries,' said the mechanic. He stepped backwards and waved. 'Fly safe!'

'Thanks, mate. See you later.'

The mechanic wandered back to the hangar to work on another plane. He knew Shane and trusted him, so he didn't bother asking any more questions.

Usually, Shane would personally check any small plane before taking off. He didn't like to put his life in anyone else's hands. Today was different. There was no time to waste. He'd just have to trust the mechanic. He started the engine. The propellers spun.

Shane handed Tim a pair of headphones, then put on a pair himself. They would protect their ears from the noise and allow them to talk to one another without yelling.

Shane spoke to the control tower, asking for permission to take off.

Five minutes later, they were airborne.

They flew out of Kingsford Smith Airport and over La Perouse. Through the windows, they could see the spindly skyscrapers in the heart of the city and, beyond them, the glorious curves of the bay. Water glistened in the sunlight, silhouetting tiny beaches, harbours and islands.

'Pretty good, huh?'

Tim nodded. 'It looks nice.'

'It's more than nice,' said Shane. 'It's beautiful.'

'I suppose it is.'

'You know, mate, I must have visited half the cities on the planet. San Francisco, Rio de Janeiro, Paris, Rome, Marrakech, Kyoto, Budapest, Venice, Dubrovnik, New York... I've seen them all. Most of them were pretty good. Some were great. But not one matched Sydney. I've got to tell you, mate, this is the most beautiful city in the world.'

Shane pointed out the Harbour Bridge and the Opera House, its curved white roofs gleaming in the sunlight. On a clear day like this, he said, they could almost see the windows of his own apartment in Surry Hills.

Shane angled the plane away from the city and towards the mountains, following the signal sent by the tracker in Red Jelly's chopper.

Below them, the city dropped away. The busy streets, densely populated with houses and cars and people, were replaced by an emptier landscape of gentle hills and dense woodland, punctuated by a few roads and houses.

Tim borrowed Shane's phone and sent a text to his mum.

He thought about ringing Max and Natascha, but decided to leave them in peace. He didn't want to raise their hopes. Not yet, anyway. Later, when he'd found Grk, he would tell them everything.

Shane took the phone back and switched it off. He didn't want the police to find its signal and follow them.

They settled in their seats and prepared for the long flight ahead.

Chapter 38

Mrs Malt liked Sydney.

She hadn't seen much of the city, of course. Actually, she hadn't even left the hotel yet. But it was a very good hotel. Her room had a comfortable bed and a luxurious shower and a large terrace with a glorious view of the Harbour Bridge. She had slept well. Her shower had been hot and invigorating. She was dressed in clean clothes. Now she was ready to meet Chief Inspector Sam Somerville and hear all about the progress of the investigation. She went to fetch Tim, who was sleeping in the adjoining room.

She knocked on his door.

There was no answer.

She knocked again.

Still no answer.

She opened the door.

The room appeared to be empty.

Mrs Malt felt a sudden lurch of panic. She hurried into the bathroom, checked the terrace and even looked under the bed.

The room *was* empty.

Tim might have been anywhere. He could have gone for a swim in the hotel pool, for instance. Or he might have wandered downstairs to see the rest of the hotel. It was quite possible that he was sitting in the restaurant, sampling the local cuisine, trying a few Aussie specialities.

But Mrs Malt knew her son better than that. If he had disappeared from his room, he must have gone to find Grk.

She pulled out her phone to call her husband and tell him what had happened. It was the middle of the night in London, but he wouldn't mind being woken up. Looking at the display, she noticed that she had been sent a text message. It had come from an unfamiliar number. She read it.

Hi mum gone 2 look 4 grk back soon please dont worry please dont follow me love from tim

Mrs Malt sighed.

'Oh, Tim,' she whispered to herself.

She read the message again and then she sighed once more.

She loved her son. Of course she did. There was no one in the world who she loved more. Not her husband, or even herself.

But why did he have to run away? Why couldn't he just tell her where he was going? And why did he have to do it here in Australia?

She knew there was no point asking these questions. Only one person could answer them and he had disappeared.

Chapter 39

A thousand miles from Sydney, Grk lay on the ground, very full, very happy and fast asleep.

He had dragged half a steak and five sausages through the dust to keep him company, but he couldn't eat another mouthful. He used them as a pillow instead. He'd have them for breakfast when he woke up.

Around him, the party got louder and wilder, but he didn't notice.

He slept through it all, dreaming about squirrels and rabbits and wombats and kangaroos and the biggest steak on the planet.

He didn't hear the shouts or the laughter. He wasn't disturbed by the stamping feet or the clapping hands or the singing. Every now and then, he opened an eye and glanced at his surroundings, checking that nothing had changed. Then he closed his eye again and went back to sleep.

As he dozed, twenty men were drinking beers and eating sausages and singing and laughing and talking and slapping one another on the back.

One of the men had twelve silver wristwatches tied to his arm. Another was wearing a necklace of two-hundred tiny pearls. A third had six diamond rings on each of his little fingers.

The Red Jelly Gang were celebrating their victory.

They had taken possession of a small town in the middle of the outback and made their camp in its main street.

The town was called Dead Dog Creek. Many years ago it had been full of people, but no one had lived here for a long time. The Red Jelly Gang had the whole place to themselves.

While the rest of the gang were robbing the Sydney Opera House, one of Red Jelly's men drove to Dead Dog Creek in a ute laden with enough food and drink to feed twenty hungry men for a couple of days. (A ute, by the way, is the Australian name for a pick-up truck.) When the four helicopters landed, he had been waiting for them with a crate of cold beers. He handed them round and demanded to know every detail of the robbery. He wished he could have been there too, but one member of the gang had to drive the truck, and he'd picked the short straw.

As soon as they finished their beers, the Red Jelly Gang pulled the black bags out of the helicopters, emptied them and did a rough valuation of their stash. They now knew that they had made the biggest haul of their lives.

Tonight, they were throwing a party to celebrate.

Tomorrow, they would divide up their spoils, climb into the ute and the four helicopters, and travel in different directions. They wouldn't meet again until Red Jelly summoned them to commit another robbery.

In the middle of the street, between the bank and the hotel, they built a big bonfire. The flames blazed for an hour or two. In the dying embers, they made an immense barbecue, stacked with sausages, ribs, chops, steaks and skewers of lamb and chicken.

They ate till they couldn't eat any more. Then they grabbed some beers and squatted in the dirt, discussing how they were going to spend their share of the loot.

Red Jelly fetched a crate from the truck and walked around his gang, handing out beers. 'Go on, mate,' he said. 'Have another tinnie. You've earned it.' He turned to the man who was standing nearest to the radio. 'Hey, Russ! Turn it up! I love this song.'

'You don't think it's too loud already?' asked Russ.

'Don't be stupid,' said Red Jelly. 'Who's going to hear us?'

'There might be someone round here.'

'There isn't,' said Red Jelly.

'How do you know?'

'This place is empty, mate. Has been for years. Might be some lizards. The odd roo. If they want to join the party, they're welcome. But you don't have to worry about anyone else. Go on, turn it up.'

Russ did as he was told. Music boomed into the air. Then he took another beer and cracked it open. 'Cheers, mate.'

'Cheers,' said Red Jelly.

They knocked their beers together and drank them down in a single glug.

Chapter 40

Arthur Hubbard peered through his dusty windscreen and rubbed his eyes. Then he rubbed them again. Was he dreaming? Or was he going mad?

He was driving back from Broken Hill. His ute was packed with enough rice, beans and beer to get him through the next month.

Now he was driving down one of the loneliest roads on the planet.

Fifty miles back, a kangaroo had bounced through the beams of his headlights. Since then, he hadn't spotted a single living creature. You could drive along this road for hours without seeing another car. You could drive for years without seeing a pedestrian.

And now . . .

Now he was dreaming. Or he was going mad. Those were the only two explanations. Why else would he be able to see four people sitting by the side of the road?

He blinked and rubbed his eyes once more and squinted through the windscreen, but the four figures didn't disappear.

When you drive for a long time through an empty landscape with no company except the radio and your own voice, you start seeing mirages. A pub pops out of the landscape. Then you blink and the vision shimmers into the dust and disappears.

These four people didn't shimmer or disappear. In fact, they stood up and waved their arms, making sure he didn't miss them.

Arthur jammed on the brakes. His heavily loaded ute lurched and screeched and shuddered before finally rolling to a halt.

Arthur opened the door, clambered out and gave the four people a long, hard stare. Then he said, 'Do you want a beer?'

All four nodded.

'You're in luck. I filled my Esky this morning. Four beers, coming right up.'

As any Aussie will be able to tell you, an 'Esky' is an Australian cool-box. Arthur kept one in his car. When you're driving down dusty roads, there's nothing better than a cold drink. He opened the Esky, lifted out four beers, and handed them round.

Arthur fetched a lemonade for himself and took a long drink. He waited till everyone else had done the same. Then he said, 'If you don't mind me asking, what are you blokes doing out here?'

Sir Tristram Tinderbiscuit and his three new-found friends all talked at once. They told Arthur about the siege. They described how four helicopters had flown out of Sydney, taking Red Jelly and his men and the big black bags stuffed with money and jewels.

They pointed to the place where the four helicopters had landed. There, the four of them had been pushed out and forced to stand in the baking heat. Red Jelly had shaken their hands, wished them luck and given them two big bottles of water.

'Don't worry,' he had said. 'You'll be safe here. Some-one will drive down the road eventually. You might just have to wait a few hours.'

Then he'd got back into his helicopter and flown away.

Since then, the four of them had been sitting under the eucalyptus tree. They'd sat there through the heat of the day and the chill of the night, listening to the strange sounds of the outback. Over the past few hours, they had begun to wonder if they were going to die right here, sitting in the shade of this eucalyptus tree.

Their water had almost run out. There was only a little dribble left at the bottom of each bottle. Another few hours and they would die of thirst.

Arthur Hubbard had heard about the siege on the radio, but he never imagined that he might find the four hostages himself. He wondered if he might earn a smidgeon of the reward. Then he told himself to stop being so greedy. He had four sickly, sunburnt people to worry about.

'You'd better get in,' he said. 'If you don't mind a squeeze, you'll all fit.'

Jimmy Hu and Rebecca Ward clambered into the front of the ute and sat alongside Arthur Hubbard. Robert Corrigan and Sir Tristram Tinderbiscuit sat in the back. Arthur started the engine and they headed for the nearest town.

Chapter 41

Tim and Shane had been flying for a little more than three hours when they found themselves directly above the tracking device.

Shane tipped the plane over on one side so he could look down at the landscape. Then he tipped it the other way so Tim could look too.

Tim saw a vast expanse of reddish earth, stretching to the horizon in every direction.

A single line cracked the landscape in half. That was a road, Shane explained. Like most roads in the outback, it probably wasn't tarmacked, just cleared of the biggest rocks.

Driving out here, you had to be careful. If you ran out of fuel, you might have to walk a hundred kilometres to the nearest garage. If you punctured a tyre and didn't have a spare, you might have to wait a month for a passing motorist.

Directly beneath them, the road went through a cluster of tiny specks. Those were houses, said Shane. A farm, perhaps. Or, more likely, a little town. If he dropped to a lower altitude, they would be able to see the four helicopters. If they went even lower, they would spot Red Jelly and his twenty men – and perhaps even Grk too.

Shane flew onwards, hoping that Red Jelly would

dismiss the plane as a farmer heading home or a tourist travelling to Alice Springs.

Shane handed a map to Tim. 'Can you open that?'

Tim unfolded the map on his knees. With Shane's help, he found their position.

According to the map, those houses were a tiny town named Dead Dog Creek. The map didn't say how many people lived there.

There wasn't an airport at Dead Dog Creek. Or even a landing strip. There was only one possible place to land a plane.

The road.

They flew onwards for ten minutes. Then Shane angled the plane towards the ground and dropped down, down, down through the sky. When they were barely higher than the tallest trees, he turned around and headed back towards Dead Dog Creek.

Below them, the earth flashed past with terrifying speed.

The noise of the engines shocked birds into flight. A flock of crows wheeled into the air and span away, screeching.

Tim gripped his seat.

The wings shuddered and screeched.

'Hold tight,' yelled Shane. 'We're going in.'

The plane drifted lower and lower.

The road was a narrow strip of hard earth, not even as wide as the plane's wingspan. Drift to the left or the right and they'd smack into a tree or a boulder.

Don't think about that, Tim told himself.

But he couldn't think about anything else.

Red Jelly had the right idea. Landing a helicopter here would be easy. You'd simply hover down from the sky and gently rest your undercarriage on the uneven earth.

But they weren't flying a helicopter. They were flying an eight-seater, twin-engined aircraft designed for landing in a normal airport with a long, smooth, well-lit runway.

Tim turned to his pilot. 'Have you ever done this before?'

'No,' shouted Shane. He had a wild grin on his face. 'But I've always wanted to!'

They were almost touching the earth now.

The wheels bumped on the rough ground. The plane lurched upwards, then thudded down. The tyres smacked onto the road, raising clouds of dust.

A kangaroo stood for a moment, staring in astonishment at the heavy object bearing down on him, then turned and bounced out of the way.

The plane smacked onto the road again. The tyres skidded, the wings wobbled one way and the other and then a wing tip scraped against the earth. It shattered in an instant, leaving a trail of debris in the dust.

Shane struggled with the controls, but the plane seemed to have a will of its own. It bucked and dipped and bounced and flung itself at the road as if it was trying to smash through the hard earth.

A tyre burst. Then another.

The whole structure groaned. Rivets popped. The

tail tipped up and the nose plunged down. Both propellers shaved the ground and disintegrated in a spray of metal.

The plane flipped over and the wings broke off and the windscreen smashed into a thousand pieces.

Chapter 42

Things look very different when you're upside down.

Things feel very different too.

All the blood rushes to your head. Your eyes are heavy. Your skull is a steel plate pressing on your brain. Your arms and legs feel skimpy and useless and hardly even attached to the rest of you.

Your body wants to fall to the floor, but it can't, because you're tied to your chair by a seatbelt.

These were all interesting sensations, but Tim knew he didn't have time to think about any of them, because he could smell fuel.

He knew what that meant.

When the plane turned head-over-heels and landed on its roof, the fuel pipe must have snapped. Fuel would be pouring out of the tank and collecting on the earth. A single spark would ignite the lot.

Beside him, Shane was asleep.

Asleep? Now?

'Shane!' yelled Tim. 'Wake up!'

That was when he noticed the blood.

It was dribbling down Shane's face, collecting on the tip of his skull and dripping onto the ceiling.

Was he dead?

No, he was still breathing. He must have been knocked unconscious by the impact.

Tim struggled again, trying to pull himself out of his seat, but he was stuck. He needed help. And he needed it before they were both blown into a million pieces.

Tim reached across and shook the pilot's arm. 'We've got to get out of here!' he shouted.

Shane groaned.

Tim yelled louder. 'Shane! Wake up! We're going to die!'

Finally Shane opened his eyes. He tried to turn his head, but the pain was too much. Then he realised he was upside down. He looked at Tim. His voice was strangely quiet. 'What happened?'

'We crashed. Are you all right?'

'Yeah, I'm fine.' Shane twisted in his seat. 'Just stuck.'

'Me too.'

'Wait a second.' Using every last reserve of strength, Shane stretched across the cabin and unclasped Tim's seatbelt. 'Can you get out now?'

Almost wrenching his arm out of its socket, Tim managed to struggle free of the strap. He turned sideways and tumbled onto the roof of the plane. His feet followed after him, thumping against the seat and the instrument panel, then collapsing around his ears.

Ow.

The pain.

No time to worry about that now.

Tim untangled himself and opened the door.

He hauled himself out of the plane and landed face-first in the dust. He would have been happy to lie there for a minute or two, inspecting his wounds, but he knew he had to save Shane first.

He hurried round to the other door and undid Shane's seatbelt. Although he tried to be as gentle as possible, he couldn't help bashing Shane's limbs against the door of the plane as he hauled him out. Shane winced, but didn't complain. He just said, 'Thanks, mate.'

'No worries,' said Tim. He'd only been in Australia for a few hours, but he already knew how to speak Australian.

'Help me up,' said Shane. 'We'd better shift our-selves. This plane might blow any minute.'

Tim was much smaller and lighter than Shane, but he somehow managed to help the bigger man to his feet.

'Does your leg hurt?' asked Tim.

'It's no problem.'

'What about your head? You're bleeding.'

'Oh, it's just a little scratch. Come on, mate. Let's make for that tree. Here, give me your shoulder.'

Shane leant on Tim's shoulder and they half-walked, half-hopped down the road towards a big gum tree.

Every step must have been agonising for Shane, but he never complained. He just winced a little every now and then as if he had a toothache.

The gum tree was about fifty metres from the road. If a car came towards them, they would see its dust from miles away, giving them enough time to hide.

On the horizon, Tim could see a few dark shapes shimmering in the haze. They could have been cars or trucks, but Shane assured Tim that those distant

165

silhouettes were actually buildings. That was Dead Dog Creek. Somewhere in the middle of those distant shapes, they would find four helicopters and twenty criminals and a small white dog.

They sheltered in the shade provided by the wide canopy of branches and discussed what to do next.

'I'm not going to be much help,' said Shane, gesturing at his leg. 'And you can't tackle Red Jelly on your own.'

'I could try.'

'No way, mate. That would just be suicide. You're a brave kid, but you can't take on twenty armed men. They'll just blow you away.'

'I've got to get Grk back,' said Tim.

'Of course you do, mate. But you don't want to die trying.'

'So what you do suggest?'

'I don't know,' said Shane. 'My phone doesn't have a signal out here, so we can't call for help. I haven't got a gun. Or even a knife. I can barely walk. And you're just a kid. I'm very sorry, mate, but I think I've landed you in the middle of a horrible mess. I should have left you with your mum.'

'No, you shouldn't,' said Tim. 'I wanted to come and help Grk.'

'You won't help him if you're dead.'

'I know,' said Tim. 'But there must be something we can do. We just need a brilliant plan.'

'I'm not very good at brilliant plans,' said Shane.

'Nor am I,' said Tim. 'But let's try and think of one.'

They sat with their backs to the tree, staring at the bleak landscape, and thought until their heads hurt.

Every few minutes, different strange noises echoed out of the bushes: a chirrup or a shriek, a cry or a warble, the noises of mysterious animals and reptiles.

Around them, there were a few signs of life: an eagle circling overhead; a snake slithering through the dust; a pair of kangaroos lolloping between the spiky bushes. But the outback mostly looked dry and dusty and worryingly dead. Tim knew that if they stayed here, leaning against this tree, without food or water, he and Shane would soon be dead too. He had to think of something. An idea. A plan. A brilliant scheme to rescue Grk from Red Jelly.

He thought through the events of the past few days. He tried to remember everything that he knew about the Red Jelly Gang. He imagined what Grk must have seen and felt. He thought about Dead Dog Creek and the bags of money and the four helicopters that had flown here from Sydney. And then he had an idea.

Chapter 43

'Tim,' hissed Shane. 'Hey, Tim, wake up.'

For a moment, Tim wondered why someone was talking to him in an Australian accent. Then he sat up and rubbed his eyes. 'What time is it?'

'An hour before dawn.'

They were whispering, although there was no need to. Even if they shouted, they wouldn't be heard by anyone except a few snakes, lizards and a couple of kangaroos.

Tim had a pee behind the tree, then they set off, walking along the road at a slow but steady pace.

Last night, before the sun set, Tim had searched the local area and returned with two long branches. Shane had torn strips from his shirt and attached one branch to his leg as a splint. Now he was using the second branch as a crutch.

Overhead, the stars faded as the first glimmer of dawn crept across the sky. Looking through the gloom at the road ahead, they could see the silhouettes of buildings, gradually growing bigger and more distinct.

They came to a signpost by the side of the road. In the frail light, they could just distinguish the black letters painted on the white board:

DEAD DOG CREEK
Population: ~~210~~ ~~93~~ ~~26~~ ~~11~~ ~~2~~ 0

'Zero?' said Tim. 'How can a town have a population of zero?'

'Everyone must have gone.'

'But where?'

'Somewhere with water, I guess. And jobs. There are a few of these towns in the outback. They sprang up during the gold rush back in the 1800s. Someone found a nugget. Other people heard about it. They came running. Built a hotel, a few houses, a church. Then the gold ran out. So everyone left.'

They carried on walking.

The sun rose just as they reached Dead Dog Creek.

On the outskirts of the town, they found four black helicopters standing in a field like horses, waiting to be ridden.

That was where they said goodbye.

They shook hands.

'Good luck,' said Shane.

'You too,' said Tim.

Without another word, they went in different directions.

Shane hobbled through the dust to the nearest helicopter. He propped his crutch against the under-carriage and swung himself into the cabin, groaning gently to himself when he knocked his leg against the door.

Tim walked briskly into Dead Dog Creek. The first beams of the rising sun lit up the roofs of the buildings. He could hear a noise which he couldn't immediately identify and then he realised it was a pop song. Who would be playing music at this time of the morning? He'd find out soon enough. He walked slowly and carefully between two houses, then poked his head round the corner and peered down the main street of Dead Dog Creek.

In fact, it was the only street.

Dead Dog Creek consisted of a single long street and a few derelict buildings and just about nothing else.

Shane was right about the gold rush. Over a hundred years ago, the small town had been built to house the sudden arrival of several thousand prospectors and miners, hoping to find enough yellow metal to earn their fortune.

The Dead Dog Creek Hotel offered them a bed for the night where they could rest their weary limbs at the end of a long day's digging.

The Dead Dog Creek Bank stored their new-found nuggets or exchanged them for paper money.

However, there wasn't much money to be made in Dead Dog Creek. The new arrivals soon realised that there was no gold to be found. They went home empty handed.

The locals had nothing to put in the bank and nothing to take out either. No one wanted to sleep in the hotel. The town emptied. A few residents stayed in their houses, scraping a living from the dry soil, and then they died or went elsewhere, and the population shrank to zero.

Since then, the bank, the hotel, the church, the school and all the other houses in Dead Dog Creek had stood here, lonely and empty, forgotten and unused, crumbling a little more every year. The windows had no glass. The doors hung open. Every roof was punctured with holes.

It was the strangest town that Tim had ever seen.

And the strangest thing was this: twenty men were sprawled in the road. Some were lying face down in the dust. Others were slumped against a wall or a tree trunk.

At first, Tim thought they must be dead. Then he realised that they were sleeping.

Their bodies were surrounded by what looked like the remnants of a wild party. Empty cans of beer were scattered everywhere, mingling with plastic plates and forks, half-eaten loaves of white bread, piles of burnt sausages and half-chewed bones.

A radio was mumbling gently to itself, playing pop songs, but the Red Jelly gang slept through the noise. They had been drinking all night and they had no reason to wake up this morning.

A ute was parked at the opposite end of the street.

Near the ute, a huge man was lying on his back in the dust, his big belly sticking out of the earth like a mountain. It was Red Jelly. He was fast asleep. And so was the little white dog who was lying beside him.

Tim stared at Grk. Finally, he'd found him. But now he didn't know what to do.

Should he creep closer? And try to attach a lead to Grk's collar? But he didn't want to get too close to Red Jelly. He preferred staying where he was, out of range of a heavy fist or a leather boot.

Then he had an idea.

He pursed his lips and whistled very quietly.

He whistled so quietly, in fact, that he couldn't even hear himself.

He tried again, a little louder.

Not loud enough to wake any sleeping criminals, but loud enough to wake a dog with very sensitive ears.

Red Jelly didn't even stir, but Grk sat up and looked around. His nostrils twitched. His ears waggled. He sprang to his feet, turning his head from side to side, searching for the source of the noise. Then he saw Tim.

For a moment, Grk couldn't believe what he was seeing. Then he barked with delight – *Woof! Woof! Woof!* – and sprinted through the dust as fast as his little legs would carry him.

'Shhh!' hissed Tim, putting his finger to his lips.

Grk took no notice. He was too happy, too excited. He sped down the main street of Dead Dog Creek, his tail wagging and his mouth open.

Woof! Woof! Woof!

Red Jelly opened his eyes. Something had woken him, but he wasn't sure what. He rubbed his big bald head with his chubby fingers. He stretched his long arms. Then he looked for Bingo.

Where had that dog gone?

He heard a noise.

Woof! Woof! Woof!

Red Jelly sat up.

That was when he saw the thief.

He couldn't believe it.

What was a boy doing here? Who was he? How had he got to Dead Dog Creek? And why did he want to steal Bingo?

Grk could have talked for hours. There was so much to say. He would have asked a hundred questions and then he would have described all the crazy things that had happened to him over the past few days. But he couldn't talk, so he simply threw himself into Tim's arms and licked the tip of Tim's nose and then barked as loudly as he could.

Woof! Woof! Woof!

Tim liked having his nose licked. He would have been happy to roll in the dust, tickling Grk's belly and messing about. But he knew they had to get out of Dead Dog Creek as fast as possible.

'Come on,' he said. 'This way.'

He turned and ran down the main street. Grk sprinted happily alongside him, his tail wagging faster than it had ever wagged before.

Red Jelly stared at the boy and the dog.

He could have run after them. But they had a head start. And he didn't like running. There were much better ways to catch people.

You could use a gun, for instance. A bullet travels fast enough to catch even the speediest sprinter.

He pulled a pistol from the waistband of his trousers and took aim.

But he didn't shoot.

173

He had just woken up and his head ached from last night's party. If his hand wobbled, he might miss that nasty little thief and hit Bingo instead. He didn't want to hurt his new best friend. He tucked his pistol into his waistband and lumbered across the street to the ute.

Red Jelly hauled himself into the driver's seat and turned on the engine. Then he pressed his fist on the horn.

A deafening PAAAAARRRRPP! echoed up and down the main street of Dead Dog Creek.

Three of Red Jelly's men slept thought the noise. The others rolled over, clutching their heads and groaning and wondering what that awful noise was.

Red Jelly pressed the horn again. PAAARRRPP! Wake up, he was saying. Come and help me. We've been attacked. Then he released the handbrake and thrust his foot on the accelerator. The wheels spun and the ute leaped forwards, leaving a cloud of dust.

The more quick-witted members of his gang understood immediately what had happened. Someone was trying to steal their new-found wealth. They sprang to their feet, grabbed their weapons and sprinted down the street in pursuit of their leader.

Chapter 44

Tim and Grk dashed across dirt and dust that hadn't felt a human foot for many years. They dodged down a narrow gap that ran between the bank and the hotel and headed for the bush.

The sun was higher in the sky now and its fierce glare shone straight into their eyes.

Tim didn't know where he was going. He just knew he had to get away from Red Jelly. He put his head down and sprinted away from the town. He didn't even glance at Grk, but he knew he didn't have to. He was confident that the little dog would be galloping alongside him, keeping up with every stride.

Behind them, there was a massive crash.

What was that? A bomb? A bazooka?

Tim knew he should keep running, but he couldn't resist the temptation to see what had exploded behind him. He glanced over his shoulder.

A moment ago, he and Grk had run down a narrow gap between two ancient buildings.

That gap no longer existed. It had been filled with bricks knocked out of the bank and the hotel.

Spilling debris into the dust, the truck was heading straight for Tim and Grk.

Through the dark windscreen, Tim could see the vast bulk of the driver, taking up twice as much space as any ordinary man.

'Run!' shouted Tim.

They couldn't possibly go faster than a truck. But they had to try.

There was a small, spindly tree up ahead. Tim dodged to the left. Grk went to the right. They met on the other side and kept running.

The truck accelerated after them.

Red Jelly hunched over the steering wheel. His eyes were wide and his hands were sweaty and he was smiling to himself.

'Come here, Bingo,' he whispered. 'Come back home.'

With an ear-shattering CRUNCH, Red Jelly's ute drove through the tree, knocking the trunk to the ground.

Through the dust and the dirt and the mess of broken branches, Red Jelly could see the boy and the dog. He headed straight for them.

Red Jelly had a sudden memory of himself, years and years ago, rolling in the dust with Bingo.

That was before his accident, of course. He hadn't been Red Jelly then. He had been Sidney O'Sullivan, a miserable kid living a miserable life in a miserable town.

He hated his family, his town and his life. But he had one good friend – a little white dog. Together, the two of them sneaked out of the town and found a quiet spot under a tree. And there, sometimes, Sidney would manage to forget how unhappy he was.

Until Bingo died. And he was left alone.

He wasn't going to let that happen again.

Bingo was back and this time, no one was going to take him away.

Up ahead, the boy and the dog peeled to the left, trying to use their agility to outwit and escape the vast truck.

Red Jelly yanked the steering wheel.

The tyres screeched in protest. The ute lurched and wobbled and finally turned a tight corner, spraying dust under the wheels and smashing through another spindly tree.

Tim knew he had only one way to escape.

He couldn't fight a truck. Or outrun it.

But he could weave and dodge and double-back.

And by weaving and dodging and doubling-back, Tim and Grk did indeed manage to gain a few moments of freedom. Then the truck was bearing down on them again, coming closer and closer.

Tim had the weird sensation that he could feel the heat of the engine on the back of his neck. This is it, he thought. I'm going to be squished like a grape under a big man's boot, unless I can run faster than I've ever run in my life. He put his head down and gulped air into his lungs and tried to find a last reserve of energy.

Then he tripped on a branch.

His ankle gave way. A bolt of pain shot up his leg. He fell forwards and landed in a heap on the ground.

The truck was almost on him.

He couldn't move. He didn't have a chance.

He closed his eyes.

Grk stared at the huge, gleaming, metallic monster that was bearing down on him, gushing black fumes.

He didn't know what it was or where it had come from.

But he knew he had to stop it.

In a second, the monster was going to trample over Tim and squash him flat.

Grk couldn't let that happen.

He whirled round, placed himself between Tim and the front of the truck, and started barking furiously, telling the monster to go away and leave them alone.

Red Jelly hardly even had time to think.

Below him, the boy was sprawled in the dust, an easy target, just asking to be flattened by the big fat wheels of this heavy ute.

But Bingo was standing right in front of the boy. He was staring up at the truck. His ears were standing upright. His eyes were bright and black and full of life.

Squash one and you'd squash them both.

Red Jelly stared through the windscreen at Bingo.

His best friend.

His only friend.

Hardly even knowing what he was doing, Red Jelly hauled the steering wheel downwards, forcing the truck to the right.

Wheels skidded, metal groaned, hinges buckled, and the heavy vehicle shuddered through an excruciating turn.

It was too much.

The ute toppled over and crashed into the ground. Red

Jelly was thrown forwards. His enormous bulk smashed into the windscreen. His head cracked against the glass. And he was knocked unconscious.

Tim didn't know where he was or what was happening to him, but he did know one thing for sure: he'd never heard such a loud noise in his entire life. The earth was screaming. His limbs were shaking. His ears were about to explode. He rolled over and sat up and wiped the dust out of his eyes, trying to see what was making all that racket.

A helicopter was landing right beside him. He could see Shane sitting at the controls, waving and yelling. It was impossible to hear what Shane was actually saying, but Tim could guess.

He pulled himself to his feet. Ignoring the pain in his ankle, he ran at the helicopter and threw himself through the open door. Then he turned round and gestured to the little white dog squatting unhappily in the dirt.

'Grk,' he yelled. 'Grk! Come here!'

Grk couldn't hear him. The rotors drowned out his voice.

A bullet fizzed through the air.

Then another.

Red Jelly's gang were coming.

Tim screamed even louder.

'Come on, Grk! Come here! Jump in!'

Grk only had a split second to make a decision, but that was enough. Given a choice between a stomach-wrenching ride through the empty air and a barrage of bullets, he knew which he preferred. He galloped through the swirling dust, hurled himself through the air and jumped into the helicopter.

He was just in time. As soon as he'd scrambled aboard, the door slid shut and the helicopter rose into the air.

A bullet pinged off the undercarriage. Another punctured the windscreen, leaving a small hole.

Shane wrestled with the controls, yanking the helicopter from side to side, trying to avoid the gunfire.

The chopper swept over trees and bushes, pursued by bullets.

Some of Red Jelly's gang kept firing at the chopper and the rest went to help their boss.

They could see his huge form inside the ute. His face was slumped against the steering wheel and his bald skull was speckled with blood. Was he dead?

They opened the door of the truck and hauled him out, pulling him by his boots and dragging him into the dust.

The bump woke him. Red Jelly sat up, clutching his head. He had been bashed and bruised and thrown around, but he was still alive. Just about. He looked at his gang and said in a deep voice, 'Where's Bingo?'

'Who's Bingo, boss?'

'The dog, you idiot. Where's my dog?'

'Over there!'

Red Jelly turned to look. He could see a distant dark speck hanging in the sky like a mosquito. With every second, the helicopter shrank as it flew further away.

He turned back to his men. 'What are you waiting for? Pull me up!'

Ten men sprang forwards, grabbed Red Jelly's arms and helped him to his feet.

His head ached. His body was covered in bruises. But he wasn't going to lie down or go to sleep. Not till he'd rescued Bingo, anyway. He wobbled unsteadily, then put one foot ahead of the other and ran towards Dead Dog Creek. His men ran with him.

Red Jelly didn't go into the town itself. Instead, he headed for the other three helicopters.

Red Jelly threw himself aboard the nearest one. A pilot jumped in after him. Other men took the back seats.

'Go!' screamed Red Jelly. 'Go! Go! Go!'

The pilot prepared for take off. He clicked switches and yanked levers. Then he started the engine.

Nothing happened.

He tried again.

Still nothing happened.

'Take off!' screamed Red Jelly. 'Why aren't you taking off?'

'I can't,' said the pilot.

'Why not? What's wrong with you?'

'There's nothing wrong with me, mate. It's the chopper.'

Chapter 45

When Tim and Shane reached the nearest town, they landed their helicopter and called the police.

'Hello,' said Shane. 'My name's Shane. I've caught Red Jelly. Do you want to know where he is?'

'You've caught him, have you?' The police operator sounded a bit tired. That day, she had talked to at least twenty people who claimed to know the whereabouts of the Red Jelly Gang. 'Where is he, then?'

'Dead Dog Creek,' said Shane.

'Oh, yes? Where's that?'

'Look on a map,' said Shane. 'But do it quickly, will you? Someone should get over there and arrest him.'

'If you don't mind me asking, how do you know it's him?'

'Three reasons,' said Shane. 'First, I'd recognise him anywhere. Second, he's got his whole gang with him. And third, right now, I'm flying one of the choppers he got from you guys.'

The police operator still wasn't sure whether to believe him, but she asked a few more questions and gradually realised that he was probably telling the truth.

Shane explained that Red Jelly and his men were stuck in Dead Dog Creek. They had no way to get out of there.

While Tim was rescuing Grk, Shane had gone from helicopter to helicopter, disabling their engines.

The Red Jelly Gang were a hundred kilometres from the nearest town and there was only one way to get there: they would have to walk through some of the driest, hottest landscape on the planet. In other words: they weren't going anywhere.

Later that day, Chief Inspector Somerville arrived at Dead Dog Creek with three-hundred heavily armed police. They were ready for a fight. They surrounded the town, their weapons drawn.

Chief Inspector Somerville was holding a megaphone. He lifted it to his lips.

'This is the police.'

His voice boomed through the air.

'You are surrounded. Come out now with your arms in the air.'

For a moment, nothing happened.

Then there was a movement between two of the old houses.

The police lifted their weapons and curled their fingers around the triggers.

Chief Inspector Somerville peered through the haze.

An enormous red figure lumbered into view. He lifted his right arm into the air and gave a cheery wave. 'Hello, mate! How are you?'

'Stop right there!' shouted Chief Inspector Somerville. 'Put your hands in the air!'

'No worries,' called out Red Jelly. He lifted both his hands into the air. 'How are you doing, Sam?'

'Pretty good, thanks,' called back Chief Inspector Somerville. 'How about yourself?'

'Not bad, thanks. Not bad at all. I suppose you want to put me back in prison?'

'Indeed I do,' said the Chief Inspector.

'Fair dinkum.' Red Jelly held out his hands, ready to be cuffed. 'Come on, then. I'm ready for you.'

A few minutes later, Red Jelly and his men had been handcuffed and taken into custody. They didn't put up any resistance. They knew there was no point. They couldn't possibly win a battle against the entire Australian Police Force. So they simply laid down their weapons and allowed themselves to be arrested.

Chapter 46

Tim and Mrs Malt said goodbye to Shane at the hospital.

He was lying in bed, his leg covered in tape and bandages. The doctors wanted him to stay in hospital for a week, but he was planning to leave tomorrow. He wanted to go out and splash some cash.

He had just been given a cheque for a million dollars.

The Bank of Australia, the Mayor's Office, the Corrigan Media Group and the Anglo-Australian Committee for International Business Cooperation had decided that Tim and Shane deserved the reward for providing information leading to the capture of Sidney O'Sullivan, better known as Red Jelly, and his gang.

Shane offered half the money to Tim, but Tim said no. Getting Grk back was good enough for him.

Mrs Malt said, 'Have you decided how to spend it?'

'I've given a good chunk to Botany Bay Air Taxis,' said Shane. 'They want a new plane to replace the one that we smashed up.'

'But what are you going to do with the rest?'

Shane smiled. 'You know, I always thought I knew exactly what I'd do if I got my hands on some serious money. I'd buy a house on the beach and waste a few years swimming and surfing. But I've changed my mind. I'm going to go into business instead.'

'What kind of business?' asked Tim.

'I'm going to be a private detective. Me and Tony Pecorino, we're going to set up our own agency. You know he got fired from the police for misusing the tracker?'

'That's so unfair!' said Tim. 'Without him, we'd never have found Red Jelly.'

'I know, mate. At least they're not prosecuting him. Anyway, we're going to start a little business of our own in Sydney. But first, I'm going to spend some of the money on a party for all my mates. My Sydney mates and my Wagga mates and all my other mates too. There'll be free beer and a big barbie and we'll dance till dawn. You're invited, Tim. And you too, Melanie.'

'That's very nice of you,' said Mrs Malt with a polite smile. She didn't like Shane very much. She blamed him for kidnapping her son from the hotel and risking his life by flying him into the outback. 'Sadly, we're going to have to say no. We have to go back to Europe.'

'Why don't you stay here for a few days? How about it, Tim? Fancy a barbie with all my mates?'

'I wish I could,' said Tim.

'Then why don't you? You like Aus, don't you?'

'I love it,' said Tim. 'But I've got to go to Stanislavia.'

'No worries,' said Shane. 'Come back soon, all right? You're always welcome here.' He stuck out his right hand. 'It's been great to see you, mate.'

'You too.'

They shook hands.

Six hours later, Tim, Grk and Mrs Malt were sitting in a Cathay Pacific aircraft, heading for Hong Kong.

The Australian government had arranged for them to travel first class again. Tim and Mrs Malt had wide seats with big armrests and very comfortable pillows.

So did Grk. He was curled up on a seat of his own, eating delicate little pieces of smoked salmon and cream cheese, licking his lips after every mouthful. He didn't want to miss a morsel.

When they arrived in Hong Kong, they changed planes and took a flight to Milan. From there, they got another plane to Vilnetto, the capital of Stanislavia.

When their plane finally landed, they had been in the air for more than twenty-four hours. Their limbs ached and their lungs craved fresh air.

They walked out of the plane, through passport control and into the arrivals lounge, where a boy and a girl were leaning on the barrier.

'Hey!' Tim waved his arms in the air, 'Over here!'

Max turned to look at them.

Natascha flung herself over the barrier and ran across the shiny white floor.

'Grk,' she cried. 'Grk!'

Grk turned his head from side to side, wondering who was shouting at him. Then he saw Natascha.

Over the past few days, Grk had travelled twenty thousand miles. He had gone all the way around the planet. Now, finally, he was back with his favourite girl in the whole wide world. And he was happy.

Grk lay down on the floor, rolled onto his back and waited for Natascha to tickle his belly.

THE grk BOOKS

When Timothy Malt finds a little white dog sitting outside his house and decides to adopt him, he little suspects what adventures he is signing up for. He flies a helicopter in Eastern Europe, exposes an international art thief in New York, and chases bank robbers through the jungles of Brazil!

WHIZZ ROUND THE WORLD WITH A GRK BOOK!

9781842703847

9781842705278

9781842705537

9781842705599

9781842706602

9781842706619